Washed UP

www.redbudave.com

WASHED UP

A NOVEL BY

TERESA SEALS

Washed UP
By
Teresa Seals

Acknowledgment

First and foremost, I want to thank GOD for the talent he has blessed me with. I'd like to thank my confidant and partner, Aaron Taylor. The past is behind us and the future is so bright. We have been down so you know what's left. Just as you are here for me and mine, I'm here for you and Alicia. Robert Ford I can't thank you enough so all that's left to say is….Let's get it in!

I'd like to thank my grandmother the sweetest woman in my world; they don't make many like you anymore. Tiara, you made mommy proud by breaking the cycle. Antonio, Trenay, Johnniece and Jaylon, you all make me proud as well; your day is coming and you all have big shoes to fill. I love you all dearly because it's you all that give me this drive and determination. My extra child Matthew you gonna have to stop sleeping on my couch. My parents: Nancy, Jimmy, Daddy and Wanda, thanks for the continuous support. Ashley and April no one can ask for betta sistas. I love you both. My one and only, Aliyah, auntie loves you. To all my family members, especially Natalie, Nicole, Ruble, and Keith I thank you for all those encouraging words. To my extended family the Taylor's: Ruthie, Janice, Ronnie, Crystal, Candice, Collette, Dana, and Veronica thanks for the warm acceptance and embrace.

To my girls and my personal "Oprah" and "Dr. Phil": Yolanda, you are a true sister, and Robin you know you always keep it 100, enough said. I know people are in our lives for a season and/or a reason and through it all, you two stand the test of time. Loyalty means everything in this world.

Pamela Williams, your guidance became a blessing; Carolyn Robinson, you have become my "other" mother in such a short time. I love you both. Mollie, Tonya B., Fran, Will, Pat Fletcher, Annette Robinson, Kim Robinson, and Kandis Hart, a prosperous opportunity awaits you. Dr. Cross thanks for the words of wisdom. Delores Spinks, Dana Watts, Sheila Brady, Errica G., Syretta Kirk, and Evelyn Lee I love the support you all have shown me. Shantana Payne, my lil sister, no one could ask for a better friend cause I know fo sho you got my back!

To my fellow authors: **Mary L. Wilson,** it's coming, do what you do and watch those shoes cause as soon as I get my money right it's on and poppin', **Brenda Hampton,** you help plant this seed, now watch it grow, **Endy,** my sister in writing, when you come to my HOOD, you gone get that red carpet treatment. **Rose Jackson-Beavers,** thanks for all you do. The wonderful ladies from my city: **Lea Mishell, Terra Little, Kristi Colvin, Allysha Hamber, Cynthia White and Keisha Ervin** I'm wishing you much success. **Londa B.** girl words can't explain my gratitude but know that there are endless possibilities. **K'wan,** thanks for the hospitality and just know you are my other favorite author; **Jason Poole,** I'm apologizing for my city, sorry; **J.M. Benjamin,** you are the "ultimate hustler" in my book; **Dennis Reed,** you bout to put STL number one on your list; and **Eyone Williams** the world awaits you.

Neicy Davis of Foxy 95.5 you made my first radio interview a breeze and thanks for supporting us locals. Vanessa Calvin of Black Vision Books, you hold it down. Stephanie Walker of BFLy Books, stay on that grind, girl. Ms. Toni don't think that for one moment that I didn't appreciate your assistance. It is and always much needed. To the Ladies of OOSA, they can either hate it or love it!

A special thanks to all of you who assisted in these efforts and you know who you are. To all those reading this thanks. Be on the lookout for **Red Bud Ave Publications.** OH, I can't forget... Big ups to all my HATERZ!!!! If you wanna know how it's done watch me do me!!!
B EZ

Chapter 1

GET IN FOOL

"Damn! This nigga ain't even a gwop getta and he got me all caught up in my feelings! He's tripping off some punk ass piece of paper with some names that he don't even know what it means. Mr. Officer got the audacity to be sitting up there trying to belittle me and shit. I have been this dudes *Bonnie* since day one!" Asia was speaking to herself and she was growing quickly with impatience waiting on her friend to come pick her up. She tried to put her mind at ease and find something else to do until her ride came. She thumbed through some sketches she designed months ago. As she decided to relax, the tooting of the horn let her know it was time to vacate her dwelling. With the horn blowing franticly, she knew instantly that was her ride and there was no reassurance needed. Asia opened her front door and Shante sat in the car looking at her as she emerged from the door. Asia was not in the car good before Shante sped off.

Hastily making her way through a residential area driving 65 miles per hour in a 35 mile per hour zone, Shante gritted her teeth and twisted her mouth tightly to the left side. Intensively biting the inner part of her bottom lip, it wasn't long before she realized she was bringing some excruciating pain to her very own lower lip. She quickly decided to slow down before she brought some unnecessary and unwanted attention to herself. She gazed out of the window. As the moonlight reflected in her side mirror, she noticed the look of distress on her very own face. Butterflies suddenly formed and the thoughts of the previous events pranced around in her head. The should haves, could haves, and would haves scenarios bounced around as well. The vision was disturbing. "Why did I let him walk pass me? I could have said something to him. I should have stood right up and stopped him dead in his tracks! How could he just walk pass me as if he never knew me? Why would he do this to me?" Those were just the few questions prancing as she was headed in the direction to get those questions answered. In a matter of time, she was going to attain some answers or someone was about to feel the pain that she was undergoing.

As her adrenaline intensified, her foot pressed the gas pedal as far as it could go. The tension was racing rapidly at a high rate of speed as if it were competing for NASCAR. The intensity-taking place within her was causing her to lose focus of reality. She was causing her palms to sweat as she held on tightly to the steering wheel of her '03 Mercedes 300 CLK and flooring the gas pedal. Shante was in deep thought of making it to her destination, to the point in which she was ignoring the fact that the intersection ahead of her had a red light. Once she snapped back to reality, she brought the car to an abrupt stop. The tires treaded the ground making a very loud screeching noise as she slammed onto her brakes.

She looked to the right of her taking a glance at her partner in crime making sure she was okay from the sudden halt of the car. Her friend was sitting there as if nothing had just taken place. She noticed Asia gazing out the passenger side window as if she were lost in her own thoughts. Asia was in her very own world of misery. She turned back to look out of the driver side window. Shante instantly became depressed as she looked out of her car window. The only scenery was a condemn building with broken glass shattered about the sidewalk. At that moment, Shante compared the neglect and abandonment she was witnessing from the derelict scenery to what she had experienced throughout her life.

"The damn light is green, girl." Asia broke the silence as she spoke nonchalantly, "You really need to calm down. It's no sense in getting all worked up now. You need to save all that until we get to where we are going. You are about to make me tell you to take me home. I got enough problems as it is. I don't need you flipping out on me. I got this all under control!" Asia patted her hand against her chest.

Shante heard everything that Asia had to say. Whatever Asia was going through, she somehow had self-control and always remained calm. At that moment, she didn't have time to be calm. Shante came out of her daze wondering why they were sitting at the intersection for so long. Shante slowly drove east on Natural Bridge Avenue, the gateway street that took you to anywhere you needed to be in the city. The street stretched for miles. It begins as Natural Bridge Avenue, but eventually turns into Natural Bridge Road. Shante never realized how long the street was until that moment. Anticipation began to battle with Shante's adrenaline. Shante wished she had taken another route because the street only made the distance further then she realized.

"You think he gone be at the club tonight," Shante asked her friend. She began to feel an uneasy feeling. Her stomach began to bubble as if butterflies were flying around faster than before. She envied the way Asia could stomach trouble. Her capabilities weren't as strong as Asia's, but she could bear a little pain. The longer she drove the anticipation of the situation was becoming unbearable for her.

Asia stared straight ahead. She answered nonchalantly, "You know that cat gonna be at the spot. He has been going there ever since you have known him! How often has he missed not being there? He walks around that place like he's the owner."

Shante kept her eyes glued to the road. She was starting to have second thoughts. Without looking at Asia she asked, "Are you nervous?"

Asia looked over at her dear friend with pity in her eyes. When Shante asked the question she already knew the answer, she was developing second thoughts and the possibility of wanting to back down. Asia looked out the window and with no emotion, her words slowly rolled off her tongue, "You either getting ready to go hard or you taking me home! Shit I know you can get gutter if need be. It got to be somewhere up in you." Asia let out a chuckle, holding back her own emotions as she began to feel around Shante's chest area as if she was determined to find her gutter-ness, "Dre just don't know how lucky he is. He better be glad I ain't get gutter with that ass!"

Shante guided her vehicle in a parking space that must have been awaiting their arrival and knew she needed to be in that exact spot. The parking space provided a perfect view to the entrance and the exit of the door of the Royal Palace. Not to mention the entrance and exit were the same door. There was only one way in and one way out for the customers. The workers had the option to use the back door of the facility in the event of an emergency. Emergencies could pop off at any moment. Most of the time, it would be someone full of alcohol and pissed off because somebody wouldn't dance with them.

In other circumstances that occasionally took place, for instance, some chic riding down on her child's father or vice-versa. If Shante's plan were to go inside, she was definitely going to make a scene having the workers use the additional exit. The crowd would disperse in fear because she was going to do something crazy to make her point. Tonight she wasn't going in. She sat in her car with her best friend in tow watching the door. The view was so perfect that they could see those who passed by the entrance and those on their way out before they even made it to open the glass door.

The Royal Place is the most popular hole in the wall lounge on the north side. It drew all kinds of crowds. The haves and the have-nots frequented this establishment. It served breakfast in the morning and some of the best shrimp dinners in the evening. Other food items like fried chicken were available, but the jumbo shrimp was on the top of the list. The drinks were watered down but the people were there to party. There was not a night of the week that the place wasn't packed. The crowd was out growing the establishment.

The DJ kept it crunk. Tonight was not out of the ordinary. The sounds could be heard for miles. During the summer and fall months, the party was usually outside on the parking lot. This parking lot would look like the strip Crenshaw, in Los Angeles on a Saturday night. This night was no different, the party would have been on the parking lot but the cold weather prevented that. The crowd always stayed until the owner locked the doors.

Shante looked over to her right. She was feeling as if she just wanted to walk in the club and make a surprise guest appearance. She quickly decided against it. She was trying to observe Asia's actions. Shante wanted to know where Asia's head was. As usual, she couldn't gather any answers just from looking at Asia. Asia thought of the most meticulous tactics, Shante never knew what Asia had in her little bag mischief. She knew that Asia had some devious tendencies but she wasn't exactly the vindictive type of person. She couldn't explain how to separate the two, but the best thing about Asia, you can tell from her actions where you stood in her life. Shante was custom to Asia's cunning ways because she had been displaying them ever since they met.

Shante was fighting with the some unexplainable feelings as she sat and watched the door of the Royal Palace. For a long time she contemplated if Asia wasn't facing her matter with Andre, could she have counted on her.

Quickly, how she came to her very own conclusion about her longtime friend. She could have kicked herself for even doubting her friend. She was dealing with her own emotions and as she juggled them both it began to interfere with her common sense. The emotional baggage she was carrying was becoming overwhelming. Her emotions began to take control. She was feeling so down but like always, Asia was there to pick her up.

Asia sat in silence because she knew why they were there. She was down for whatever because she came to do what she had to and eliminate Shante's problem. She knew that Shante may show a sign of weakness but she was prepared for whatever came first. Asia began to lay her head back against the headrest. She knew that she had to do something different. She sat there in Shante's car thinking about pursuing a dream of her own. Her thought was interrupted by the sigh Shante abruptly made. Asia thought to herself that she could hear the sounds of Shante's blood boiling. Asia just ignored Shante's body language. She knew she could relax a bit because as soon as it look like their prospect was about to emerge from out the door, Shante would let her know.

The situation had occurred just as they assumed. He was there. As usual, he exited the club before the last call for alcohol. He strolled out the club as if everyone needed to call him Mr. Royal Palace. Had he known what type of night he was in store for, he would have probably made the choice to take that last drink. Then, on the other hand, had he been the owner, the security guards would have walked him to his car because tonight he was going to need it. Because he was not the owner, he was alone and nothing was about to save him.

Shante elbowed Asia. She jumped from her designer thoughts. They watched their prospect as he stumbled toward his car that was parked approximately three cars over from where they were parked. The girls made their exit from the car quickly and quietly with the Louisville slugger and department issue Berretta in tow without notice.

Before he could react, he was brought to his knees from the blow of the Louisville slugger. He began to crawl to save his life but the hands that began to pull him were taking him in the opposite direction. Shante pulled him and Asia kicked him. He looked up into Asia's eyes. Asia looked right back at him letting him know that it was not a game.

"Get yo punk ass in the trunk, Willie." Asia pointed the Berretta directly in his view, "Now you can play like Superman and think you are faster than a speeding bullet, but I am going to play the big bad wolf and blow all that shit away." Asia wiggled the Berretta around.

He was ordered to get in the trunk of the car one last time and Asia said it with authority, "Stop looking around and get in the trunk!"

Willie sighed as he to a look down toward the trunk. Then without further hesitation, he crawled into the trunk and was trying to figure out why was this happening to him. Why was Shante acting out and taking it out on him? What scared him the most was that Asia had a tool that made him do as he was told. He wasn't sure if she knew how to use it and today he didn't want to be the guinea pig. He was lost for words. He simply couldn't utter a word. The girls were totally blowing his high. Being at gunpoint made him simply obliged without putting up a fight with the two females he knew he could handle. He got himself right in the trunk without putting up a fight. He was barely dealing with the excruciating pain from the stroke of the bat.

He was lying cramped in the trunk of Shante's silver Mercedes 300 CLK, not knowing his fate. The trunk space was limited so he couldn't move to make himself comfortable. He was tucked away like a fetus in the womb and was feeling a bit uncomfortable in the trunk of the 300 CLK. All of a sudden, he realized the very reason why he could be in this situation. "How could I be so stupid?" He thought about the past events and wished he could turn back the hands of time, but it was too late. He knew all his lying had finally caught up with him. For the last four years, he had been deceiving everyone he was involved with. Not in a million years did he ever believe that he would be caught and placed in position that he didn't know how to get himself out off. He tried to kick his way out of the trunk but he could not move. He was totally crammed and limited to minimal movement. Tonight he found himself in a situation that he never thought he'd be in. Shante was the last person on the face of the Earth he thought would ever try to bring destruction to his world. There was nothing she wouldn't do for him and she never questioned anything that ever went on.

The sounds of screeching tires on pavement were all that was heard. Five miles down the road sirens flared. Shante pulled over as they waited on the officer to make his move. Sounds of someone beating in the trunk escaped through the car.

Shante looked over at Asia wondering what to do next. Asia took a deep breath and exited the car. The officer watched as she approached him. Nasty thoughts filled his head as Asia swayed her way over to the patrol car.

"Good evening Officer Dixon. Can you tell me why are you pulling me and my friend over?" Asia stood waiting on his response. The officer wore a slight smile as the exotic thoughts dancing like sugarplums began to fade away the closer she leaned in the window of the patrol car.

"I must say I apologize and say my hellos to the future Mrs. Townsend." Officer Dixon couldn't think of Asia's name, he just knew she was a dispatcher at the main precinct and engaged to one of his coworkers.

Officer Dixon continued with a smile, "Well, I stopped you guys because you were driving extremely fast and swerving at the same time. You ladies seem to have had too much to drink I see."

Asia smiled, "Just celebrating my big day to come." She wiggled her left hand in his face exposing her engagement ring.

"I see, congratulations and drive carefully. You girls be

sure not to get into any trouble while having too much fun. Goodnight!" Officer Dixon smiled.

Asia walked back to the car as if she was on the runway and the officer watched the show with no problem. He bumped his sirens three times and both girls gave a wave as he drove off.

Willie was tucked away in the trunk, hearing the sirens. The sound made his eyes light up like a kid on Christmas morning. In all his riveting pain, he began to kick and scream as much as he could.

Asia opened the door to grab the bat. "Pop the trunk!" Asia instructed Shante as she walked to the back of the car.

He rose up about to make an exit out of the trunk and Asia shoved him with the bat, "Lay yo cheating ass down and quit crying like a little bitch!" She shoved the bat in his chest and into his stomach. The last strike was near his head, but the bat landed on his hands as he cradled his head in both of his hands.

Asia was not whom he expected to see. Colliding with the bat again was not what he wanted either. He laid down praying that the night would end and he would remain alive.

Once Asia silenced the noise, she made her way back inside the car. When Asia sat back down in the car, she gave Shante a look that let her know everything was cool. Shante pulled off into the traffic with an unknown destination with the love of her life in the trunk of her car trying to determine his destiny.

Chapter 2

SHANTE

"Willie, are you just about ready? We are always the late ones when we are meeting Andre and Asia." Shante sat on her black leather sofa. She was growing very impatient, but it really didn't matter how late they were. She would defend Willie to the end and blame everything on herself. He knew she would do just that.

Asia had a passion for being on time, which was one of the many habits she picked up from Andre. He lived by the motto, "If you get there at the time assigned, you are already late. Being somewhere at least fifteen minutes before schedule meant you were on time." Shante wasn't getting anywhere but five minutes in that time frame and Willie wasn't much different. She wondered how Willie's colleagues admired his success. Shante knew it had nothing to do with his promptness, but he did have damn good job performance in and out of the bedroom.

Willie was the only one she came across that she figured could keep her in check. She was happy to have him on her side. Whenever they were together nothing but laughter and love filled the air. Mutually, they blew off steam that lifted each other's sprits and put all their troubles in check. She found herself putting Asia on the back burner and putting Willie first when something outrageous happened and she needed some support. She nearly thanked him every day for his presence in her life. She wouldn't trade Asia for the world, but Andre physical capabilities out ranked it all. For the past fifteen years, Asia and Shante formed an unbreakable bond. This personal relationship was built on pain. From the first time they ever met, there was no separating them. These two young ladies shared the same dreams and desires. Shante could never forget when Asia told her that she would rather die before she would ever deceive her. Their friendship went beyond the definition of friend that most would find in the dictionary.

Willie smiled when he entered the room letting her know that he was ready. Outside he held the door open to his black Escalade. This was Brown & Davis Accounting LLC gift to him for maintaining the title, "Accountant of the Year" for three years in a row. He was looking to make partner very soon.

Andre and Asia entered the *Elegant Diner.* The name was an understatement. This luxuriously bistro and bar catered to the upscale movers and shakers. There were two dining areas. The first is quiet and away from the action and the other is in the midst of everything. Most didn't know about the private wine cellar dining area that Willie had made reservations for. The cellar was tucked away in the lower level of the restaurant. It set the scene for love. Burning flames of the fireplace and several votive candles dimly lighted the room. Wine racks divided the room as if they were walls with all types of wine in them.

Asia looked around in amazement. The maitre d' asked would they like to wait on the rest of their party or be escorted to their seats. Before they could make their decision, Willie and Shante had entered.

Asia and Shante were dressed for the occasion. Accidentally they both sported Vera Wang. Asia looked stunning in her black silk jacquard dress as Shante was stopping the show in her black halter pleated dress. Andre unbuttoned his suit jacket while he pulled back the chair as he waited for Asia to take a seat. Willie did the same for Shante.

"In all the time, I didn't know that you played football and basketball during high school. Shante was telling me on the way over." Willie made small talk as the ladies took their seat.

"Man you caught me off guard with that. I thought you were getting ready to tell me it's hard out here for a pimp." Andre laughed along with the girls. He always joked with Willie on how much he resembled DJ Paul from the group, *Three Six Mafia*.

"I was telling Shante when the play offs come on, I'll be glued to the tube! She said that you would be, too." Willie waited on Andre's response.

"Yeah! Asia already knows." Andre nodded his head in agreement.

Asia and Shante looked at their menus.

"What team do you think is going to make it to the championship?" Willie looked at Andre.

Andre smirked, "Dude, you already know I am rooting for the San Antonio Spurs. I know they are going to take it all the way. Your Pistons are going to be watching from the side line."

Frustration was about to grow and it was almost heard in Willie's voice as he was making his comeback statement, "I think the Pistons have the best starting lineup. Plus, we got yo boy, from the San Antonio Spurs. Besides they ain't won anything in the last nine years!"

Andre noticed Willie's frustration. Andre figured they

were just having a friendly conversation and there was no need for Willie to be getting uptight. Andre gathered his thoughts carefully before he spoke, "Dude, this is the Spurs' year! Although, the Pistons got Nazr he ain't no Ben Wallace but with the rest of the Piston's starting lineup, they might have a stronger chance in winning."

Willie couldn't tell where Andre was coming from. Willie was just a Spurs fan seconds ago. He couldn't be jumping on the Piston's bandwagon that quickly, he thought. Willie had to let Andre know that the team he was rooting for was the best pick, "The Pistons go hard. The Pistons have that home court advantage and they know how to bring their "A" game on the road."

Andre was about ready to bring this conversation to an end. He was feeling like Willie had no clue and was just making small talk. He looked around for the waitress. Turning back to face Willie, "Well the Spurs coach, Gavin Popovich, has proven to be successful. Putting Ginobili, Parker, and Duncan as his starting lineup, shit I don't have to say anymore. The less said speaks measures."

Asia could sense that Andre was getting tired of Willie's conversation. She knew Andre really didn't care for Willie. He always told her that it was something that wasn't right about him but he couldn't put his finger on it. The nonchalant tone in Andre's voice let Asia know it was time for the sports commentary to end.

Asia as she sat next to Andre, looking directly at Willie. She had to let Andre know she knew that he was growing tired of Willie's small talk. She thought of something stupid to say, "I keep telling Andre he needs to stop sleeping on Denver. Laurence Maroney gets it cracking." Everybody looked at her as if she were stupid because Laurence played football for the New England Patriots.

Willie looked at Andre then to Asia, "He plays football and we were talking about basketball!"

Asia snaked her neck, "My bad."

If Willie had been paying attention to Asia and Andre's facial expression he would have known that stating something ridiculous were her intentions. The waitress came just in time. She apologized for taking so long while informing them that some kinks needed to be worked out in the kitchen. The waitress smiled as she told them that the goat cheese, crostini, packed with fried sage leaves and roasted red pepper with a little the zest would be a nice choice.

The waitress smiled and continue to take pride in the menu, "The house-made wild boar ravioli with a spicy tomato herb ragout is a winner." She continued telling them to avoid the colossal and underwhelming pork tenderloin and instead go for the braised rabbit paired with creamy polenta. She highly recommended the gooey butter cake with a glass of wine letting them know that it was better than mom's was.

Andre, Asia and Shante were all thinking to opt for burgers and fries but instead they chose the rabbit. Willie didn't have a problem with the choice of dining, rather he liked it or not, he grew immune to making himself fit in any equation. He had chosen the locations because his colleagues spoke of it all the time. They only frequent the establishment because of the wine was like being refilled like sodas at Apple Bee's.

Dinner was over and Shante was back at home. She let

Willie know how much she enjoyed her candlelight dinner. He reimbursed her appreciation with a token of his love and an outstanding job performance. He gently caressed every tender spot of her brown skin. Shante had no idea of what heaven felt like but she believed that Willie was giving her a sample of it. This was a feeling that she felt often when Willie placed his hands upon her.

Every time Willie would enter her essence, she never wanted him to leave. The moment he asked her to bare his children she was not reluctant in her answer. She wanted to be his first, his last, and his everything else. She found pleasure in his intellectual conversation and the physical agility in the bedroom only sealed the deal.

The pressure was on when Asia told Shante how Andre came to her job to propose to her. Andre told Asia that her loving had spoiled him. He continued with how he caught himself smiling for no reason when he thought of her. Andre bent down on one knee looking on to Asia's coworkers telling them how good it feels to know that he has someone to accept him for who he is. He looked into Asia's eyes telling her that this type of love only happens once in a lifetime and he could never find himself loving another as much as he loves her. He pulled out this baguette diamond ring while asking for her hand in marriage. She cried while telling him yes. Some of her coworkers cried along with her as others applauded. When Asia informed Shante of this it only intensified her envy.

Shante's proposal went a little differently. She was so envious about Asia, Shante had to make Andre's proposal to Asia the topic of her conversation with Willie. He finally gave in one night and proposed to Shante. This was only the beginning of the rollercoaster ride and the drama was a split second away. Willie failed to mention one thing; he was in the process of reconciling with his readymade family.

~ 25 ~

Chapter 3

THICKER THAN MOST

"Wake up! Wake your lazy butt up! I see you are just a couch potato that's going to work at MC Donald's the rest of your life! Wake up! Wake up now!"

Asia rolled over to hit the snooze button on the annoying alarm clock that Andre had ordered from the home shopping network. She began rolling back over with a master plan in thought. The mission was to cuddle right up under Andre to warm up for a few more minutes and get a quickie in before she began her day. Asia's sex drive was always on high frequency.

High-quality penetration kept her coming back for more. Andre was equipped with all the right tools. A head game that made you see the sun right along with the stars and a pipe game that Mr. Rooter Rooter couldn't provide on the easiest plumbing problem. Asia wasn't going anywhere else for her tune-up. His sex game didn't have her like that in the beginning. He had all the right tools but lacked the expertise. As the bond grew stronger in their relationship, the sex became intense.

Her planned mission had failed. The wetness coming from the sheets from the previous rendezvous sent chills through her body. "How icky!" she thought. Andre laid sound asleep. The last thing she could remember was him yelling, "You love this! Tell daddy it feels good!"

He had put her ass to sleep. This was not out of the

norm for Asia. The sex was so good her insides became nearly raw on each occasion. As she creamed to her climax, she wanted to tell him to stop, but she loved the way he made her feel. No one could compare. Asia felt as though their souls were as one. Asia loved the way Andre could make her kitty-katt purr.

Asia hopped out of bed and ran to the shower. She didn't want to be late for her hair appointment. Her car was prepared for take-off once she was outside.

"Good morning, St. Louis! The time is eight nineteen. The temperature is twenty-one degrees on this Monday morning. So wrap up and wrap up those babies. You're listening to the Dee Lee Morning Show with you boy JT and ya girl E-bizzy. We are going to take a few more calls." announced the voice from the radio.

Asia pushed CD on her radio and Jeezy came through the speakers. She nodded to the beat of, *I Put on for My City* as glanced over to the patrons at the gas pumps running back to jump in their cars as the gas pumps did their jobs solo. She turned the radio down in her silver Lexus coupe and picked up her cell phone to place her call. Asia prepared herself for the lie she was about to tell.

"Good morning, Sergeant Reeder speaking. How may I direct call?"

"Good morning Sergeant Reeder, this is Asia." She gave a strong cough, "I won't be in today. I'm feeling a little under the weather." Asia lied.

"Are you getting nervous? Got those wedding day jitters?" Ms. Reeder laughed, "We figured you'd be taking some time off getting ready for that big day in all."

"It's barely two weeks away. I am so nervous. He and his family are moving my things in his house this weekend. I will be in tomorrow. The weekend just wasn't long enough."

Asia listened to her superior's congratulations as she ended her conversation.

Proceeding toward her destination, she cut the volume down because the CD began to skip. With no patience in ejecting the CD to clean it, she hit the FM dial.

"St. Louis we are still taking your calls. If you are just tuning in, we are talking about what if you found out that yo gal was just like a door knob." The radio personality's laughter intensified Asia's interest.

The male personality continued, "My boy's cousin found this list of guy names in his gal's dresser drawer while his cousin was over there picking him up. They were trying to figure out what the list meant and to make a long story short my boy told his cousin that his gal was like a door knob, everybody has had a turn."

"His ass shouldn't have been snooping around her stuff!" the female personality commented.

"Fella's, my question to you is, "If you found out yo gal had a lot of miles on her would you wife her or kick her ass to the curb? Callers, we are taking your calls right now!" Asia thought to herself, how dim-witted that topic was. She didn't want to hear another segment.

The radio personalities' voices were silenced as Asia put her CD back in and the Kanye West vocals came through the speakers as he was telling how he lost the only girl in the world that knew him best.

Asia pulled onto the parking lot of Fat Mack's Bar-be-cue joint. She looked over at the green Ford station wagon that had pulled alongside her. Placing the lip balm on her heart shaped lips; she pulled down the sun visor and lifted the compartment that concealed the mirror. She rubbed her finger over her perfectly arched eyebrows, turning to the left checking out the length of her auburn tinted hair, she ran her hand over her caramel complexion puffy cheeks. If it weren't for her caramel complexion, one would think she was the genius behind Baby Phat clothing.

Her hand stopped at her right cheek dimple as she rolled her deep chocolate slanted eyes admiring her beauty and blew herself a kiss. Asia looked down at the pug she was carrying, "I need to quit eating junk and do some damn sit ups! My stomach is starting to stick out more than my booty." Asia let the window down to test the temperature. She thought that she could dash to the door without taking her coat. Pressing the button so the window would come back up fast, she waited until it reached the top before she cut the car off. She was not emerging from the car without her coat.

Asia was out of the car entering the door of the African Braiding Station. She was about to get her hair styled with micro braids for the very first time. This was the most convenient hairstyle she could think of. She believed that it would really be convenient for the honeymoon.

After sitting for eight hours, she looked in the mirror, pleased with the braids and believed that was two hundred dollars well spent. The tightness of the braids being placed up in a ponytail had her looking like a caramel China doll. She grabbed her things to leave. Asia was so glad that the young lady was finish with her hair. She grown tired of the conversation between the women.

She wished she had paid attention in her French class during high school. When the women who opened the door, all Asia heard and could make out was "Zero, un, deux, trios, and quatre." She knew that she had just counted the five females that came through the door. Anything beyond numbers and bonjour Asia needed translation.

When Asia reached the car, she was glad that she had the auto start because the car was already warm. The temperature had dropped tremendously. She called Andre and the phone went straight to voicemail. Asia just wanted to let him know that she was going home instead of going to his place. She figured she had approximately 12 days until the wedding and four days left to be in her own home. Trying his number again with no answer, she called Shante next.

"Speak!" Shante answered with attitude.

"Did I catch you at a bad time?" Asia wanted to hang up immediately as the familiar sound came through the receiver. Hearing Shante's voice, Asia could sense something was wrong.

"I have had a bad day! No, my day has been really fucked up!" Shante paused.

Asia was afraid to ask what happened due the agony she heard as it seeped in between the attitude of her best friend's voice. This was making Asia recall the time when Shante called her to tell her about her cousins Tyrone and Keith. It brought the memory of Asia wanting to know why Keith and Tyrone were even at Shante's house when they made it obvious they didn't care much of her.

Shante's house was next to an empty lot. The lot was

occupied with a couple of used mattresses and majority of the neighborhood boys along with Keith and Tyrone would be having their own form of gymnastics taking place. Keith and Tyrone were up to something conniving as usually when they approached Shante.

Asia could always sense something was wrong with Shante and today was no different. When Shante was undergoing what Asia considered a life-changing event, her voice would tremble as if she were holding back her tears.

This was a sound that Asia dreaded hearing from her friend. Shante was not the strong one in this friendship, but with Asia by her side, she didn't need to be strong. Asia had that department covered from the first day they met.

Asia came outside looking for her cousins Keith and Tyrone. She heard a bunch of laughter coming from across the street. She followed the sounds of laughter. She noticed several neighborhood kids turning flips on dirty mattresses and Keith and Tyrone were amongst them. There were a few girls standing in the alley playing with a jump rope.

This attractive brown skin girl was sitting back taking in all the laughter. Every once in a while she would scream at whom Asia thought to be her little sister.

"Shannon you can't go in the house. You know momma said stay out here till she tells us to come in!"

The little girl backed away from the house and continued to play. Asia walked over and sat next to her. It was obvious she was in some type of pain. Not the pain of aching body parts, but the pain that displayed sorrow. Asia had been on this road a minute and she could notice this type of pain from a mile away. So going over to console this girl was so easy. A true friendship formed immediately between the pretty-brown-skinned girl and Asia. For a long time Asia yearned for the certitude of loyalty but was often disappointed. That day she didn't realize she finally found what she had always yearned. This was the beginning to a lifetime of friendship. Together they both realized later that they found a friend in each other.

Shante didn't have the strength to tell her what happened. It puzzled Asia and she wanted to know what her cousins could have done to her best friend to upset her so. She knew if she waited long enough Shante would eventually tell her and she did just that. Asia became livid when she heard the grossing details about what Keith and Tyrone had done to her friend and the pain she could hear coming through the phone now made all those bad memories resurface.

Asia held the phone waiting on Shante to speak. In a matter of seconds, she knew Shante would be pouring her heart out, it never failed in all the years they had known one another. Shante thought about the events that had taken place earlier that day and began to tell Asia.

Shante opened the door to her '03 silver Mercedes 300 CLK. As she sat down and loosened up her black leather coat, her cell phone rang. She pushed the button on the phone and spoke, "What it do?"

"I need you to go by the clinic and pick up Phat Daddy's prescription for me." Shannon said as she smacked and popped on a piece of chewing gum.

"I am the aunt not the daddy! Why can't yo baby daddy go pick it up, Shannon?"

"Some kind of sister you are. Besides this baby has a temperature that just won't break and he needs some Motrin." Shannon kept popping the gum.

"Some Motrin! You can buy that shit over the counter! I told you that you shouldn't have had that baby by that bum ass dude anyhow. Any real man a be out there stealing that shit." Shante laughed.

"Are you going to do it or not?" Shannon didn't want to hear her putting her piece of a man down.

"Where do I have to go to get this prescription?" Shante asked.

"Over on Lindell and Sarah at Health Care for Kids. Thank you Shante." Shannon hung up the phone before her sister could let another word out.

Shante pulled on the parking lot and looked at all the people walking by all bundled up. Winter could be deadly and the outside view was a homicide waiting to happen. To buy some time from leaving out of her car into the cold, she called her mother to see if she needed anything from the grocery store.

"Just bring me a fifth of Crown." Shante hated feeding her mother alcohol, but it kept her mother mellow so when she asked for it, she bought it.

Ending the call with her mother, she proceeded in to the doctor's office. She went past the waiting area straight to the receptionist desk. Shante's thickness was flamboyant. Her being knock-kneaded with a slight slew footed action going on with her right leg made her runway walk impression come off with sex appeal. When she stood up her legs appeared to go back in a stance that most men just thought was too sexy.

Brown Suga is what most people called her and she was just that. Her complexion was equivalent to brown sugar. Her hair was dark brown, tapered in the back and short and styled nicely. She had worn this hairstyle since she had entered high school. Each and every last one of her features was evenly proportioned. Small ears, piercing brown eyes, and her petite pointed nose fit perfectly with her warm smile.

Shante had worked in collections for a prestigious department store since high school. She was now a manager and head of her department. Her involvement with an accountant really didn't matter. Her bonuses, at the end of each month, put her salary near Willie's pay range.

The receptionist looked at her computer and talked on the phone as she ignored Shante's presence. Behind the receptionist was an area that gave a perfect view of where the doctors sat to view the files before entering the patient's room. This area was wide open and a few children were able to run around and play. The receptionist yelled out toward the waiting area looking right pass Shante, "Johnson, room seven!"

Shante looked back seeing the young mother gathering her diaper bag and baby seat. The door on the left side of the desk had the even numbered rooms and the door on the right had the odd numbered rooms. Shante notice that only part of the number seven was being displayed on the door. Instead of pointing to the door, Shante walked over to the door and held it opened for the young mother. It was obvious with the seven missing she didn't notice the pattern of odd on one door and even on the other door.

Always being told, patience is a virtue, Shante began to grow tired of waiting and the professionalism she was trained to use was about to go out the window. With a couple of ums and the clearing of her throat, turning around to let the receptionist know her patience had run short, she spotted a familiar face.

Asia was growing tired of Shante's commentary. She sat patiently listening to her give the play-by-play details, but her mind began to drift. She really wanted her to hurry up and get straight to the point. She could remember the first time when Shante painted the picture of the story she was trying to tell. When Shante would hear strange sounds coming from her mother's bedroom, she would imagine the wildest things. Most of the time, she would envision her and Shannon on the Screaming Eagle roller coaster at Six Flags. She imagined the screams of the roller coaster being from those who were either scared or excited. She couldn't tell if her mother was afraid or happy from the sounds she made.

Asia believed that being a collections agent was not her calling. News reporting was more of her character. Sometimes in reminiscing, Asia would start off saying, "Remembering that time when we did…." and Shante would chime in and tell the story with Asia. They were always in tuned with one another.

Shante had taken a glance of the familiar image. It was very sudden and very quick. He had entered and exited her vision so hastily that she barely took good a look at his face. The back of his head was exposed as he chased a small figure in the opening of the area directly behind the receptionist that Shante had become impatient with. All kinds of agitation and disturbance of some strong feelings ran fiercely through Shante's mind, making her adrenaline bubble.

Shante stepped away for the play-by-play commentary, "Every woman knows her man, especially, when he takes care of his business. Having a man like Willie to lay pipe the way he does, I know what that comedian meant when she said she could point her man out in the Million Man March." Shante went on to tell Asia that she could identify him with her eyes closed. Together they shared a laugh. Asia knew exactly what she meant by that because she could make Andre out with her eyes closed, too.

Reliving the event as she told her friend about what seemed to be a tragic event in her life Shante envisioned the male figure with her eyes were glued on him. She watched as he picked up the small child. She suddenly began fighting with some mixed up emotions that had her very confused. Feelings of fatigue start to consume her. She began praying it was not the man that entered her temple last night and who she had not heard from since. Now at this very moment that person who made her so happy was the same person who had her feeling so horrible earlier today because he seemed to be missing in action when she had phoned him several times. Now she was feeling even worse, seeing him standing in front of her with this child. Her favorite singer, Mary J. Blige, came to mind. She was wishing that his friends had been able to tell her about his hidden secrets. The only difference was no one knocked on her door to tell her about a child. She walked right into it. She was the one trying to deal with some understanding. This entire situation was messing her up and she stood their facing this reality not knowing what to do next.

Once he spoke and she heard his voice, it confirmed every doubt she had. She listened attentively to him saying, "Daddy got you!" The figure she had been observing turned around and there he stood standing in her view looking like looking like the rapper DJ Paul from Three Six Mafia with a young boy in his arms. Shante finally made direct eye contact with the person she was desperately trying not to believe she was seeing.

"Excuse me Ms.! Excuse me Ms.!" The receptionist spoke obnoxiously as if she hated her job to assist Shante to snap back to reality. Once the receptionist saw that Shante had focused her attention to her, she asked, "Hello, what did you say you were here for?" From Shante's look of distress, the receptionist could sense that there was a problem that had taken place. She just didn't know what it was. Her look displayed the type of look one makes when they hear a close loved one has departed from life.

Shante stood in disbelief. Her brown skin became flushed. The fullness of her lips began to look thin as they began to wear a tight frown, the seductive round brown eyes blurred as she tried to hold back the tears. Although she was saddened and deeply heartbroken, it didn't take away from the five star chic status she worked hard to maintain.

For the last four years, Willie had been so adamant about her having his first child. He had claimed that he hadn't found that special someone and since he finally found it with Shante, he felt it was time to plant his seed. Shante had convinced him that marriage would come before a child and since her best friend was getting married in February she decided that she would have a summer wedding in that same year.

Shante shook it off telling herself that was not her fiancé holding someone's child. "I am here to pick up a prescription for Caleb Irby." Shante's voice trembled as she spoke.

The receptionist grabbed a blue plastic box from the shelf that sat above her computer. Looking through the box, she came across Caleb's prescription. She handed it to Shante as she asked her was there anything else. The receptionist wanted to ask what the matter was, but she refrained from the question. She simply knew it would be best. Shante let her know that was it. She grabbed the prescription, walked away, and took her a seat in the waiting area. She sat right in the chair facing the door that Willie would have to exit when leaving the building. She hoped so anyway.

Shante turned around looking out the window noticing the sun began to disappear. She glared down looking at her left hand. She began to massage the pear shaped diamond with her right thumb. Being distracted from her thoughts by the ringing of her cell phone, she answered, "Hello."

"Shante, have you gone to pick up Phat Daddy's prescription?" Shannon asked. She was trying to see if she was going to have to something different in regards to picking up Phat Daddy's prescription. Shante had never disappointed her before when it came to doing something for her son. Shannon knew one day that she was eventually going to run it in the ground. She just hoped that this wasn't the day that Shante would grow tired of assisting with her son. Shannon just didn't understand that although Shante would put up a little fuss, she would never get tired of looking out for her and Phat Daddy.

"Yeah and I am still here. Girl, I think I just saw Willie." Shante whispered. She knew it was him, but she wanted so badly not to believe it.

"Why would his raggedy ass be at a clinic that's solely for kids? They can't help that raspy voice he has. Besides, he ain't got any damn kids!" Shannon spoke being unaware if her statement was correct as she tried to console her sister. From what she knew about him, he didn't have any children.

"I thought my eyes were playing tricks on me but then I heard his voice..." Shante responded in search for some comfort to what she was feeling.

"Did he see you?" Shannon couldn't wait on her sister to answer.

"He looked directly at me." Shante held back her pain. "Just like I know I saw him, I know he saw me as well."

"What did he do?" Shannon asked. Shannon and Shante didn't have the bond that most sisters have. She wasn't upset that Asia was closer to her sister than she was. Asia treated her like a little sister anyway. She looked up to her big sister and Shante's pain had always been Shannon's pain. Shante was a big sister who took care of her better than her very own mother. When their mother would become enraged by the pettiest events and went on a rampage, Shante would hold Shannon tight letting her know she was going to be all right.

"He acted as if he didn't know me." Shante spook with skepticism.

"Well maybe it wasn't him. They say everybody has a twin. He cares too much about you not to tell you he has a child." Shannon was trying to console her because she could hear the pain in Shante's voice. Shannon really didn't know what to say to her sister. She wasn't use to consoling her. The shoe had always been on the other foot.

Just as Shante was about to leave the door opened, a little, boy who look to be around eight years old came out the door followed by a raspy voice, "Lil Will, you better wait on me!"

"Okay Dad! I am just standing by the door," the child answered.

Then Willie exited the door holding a small child as a very hippie short woman held the door open for him, "You want Mommy to carry you?" The baby reached for the woman and Willie handed the baby off as he looked directly into Shante eyes.

In the midst of her conversation, Shante took a very long pause. The pause had Asia alarmed and puzzled. She had been listening to the play-by-play details that she almost forgot what she was waiting to hear.

"Shante! Hello! Shante, are you still there?" Asia yelled being concerned about her friend and what she had to be going through.

Shante was caught up in her thoughts. She put her hand on her head thinking it would stop the hurt that she was undergoing.

Asia began to get butterflies as she was fighting with some mixed emotions herself. She was feeling her friend's pain right along with her own. She began to wonder why Andre's phone was going straight to his voice mail. Andre had never given her a reason to think about any infidelity but neither did Willie show any signs.

"Shante, I'm staying home tonight. You know my shoulder is always there." Asia didn't know what else to say. She just knew that she would comfort her close friend in her situation.

Every since they were kids Asia had been there for her. Shante desperately yearned for someone like Asia. Although Shante's mother never left her, it felt like she did. They were in the same house together but Shante's mother never had any patience for children. Shante could remember when her mother came out of nowhere and told her she should have aborted her whenever she had the chance.

The statement hunted Shante but she never let those words affect the way she felt about her mother. She couldn't explain why her mother seemed so heartless. There had never been any physical abuse taking place, but the malicious words that rolled off her tongue leaving some detrimental scars. Shannon never experienced the word attack, but she always there to witness it.

When Shante met Asia, it brought some type of relief. Asia gave her the hugs that she needed and the love that a mother would give her only child. Asia promised that she would die before she would ever hurt her or ever see her hurt. The first day Shante ever heard Asia say that, was the last day she let anything her mother said to her make her cry.

Her mother's humiliating torture was the sole reason she focused on her five-star status and appearance. She thought it could possible hide what was always taking place inside of her.

Chapter 4

ASIA

Andre rose up and sat on the side of the bed. Asia opened her eyes and watched him seductively as he stood up and walked into the bathroom with major self-confidence. Andre was cut-up and looking like the new David Banner in every way. She admired her chocolate drop as he leaned over the sink throwing water on his face. In eight more days, she would be Mrs. Townsend.

As the phone rang, she turned to answer and Andre shut the bathroom door.

"Hello!" Asia spoke.

"It's been four days and I still haven't heard from Willie. Now when I call his phone it says out of service. I have been going pass his apartment and his car has not been on the parking lot. I have even staked out his apartment for a full twenty-four hours and he hasn't shown up yet," the stress poured through the receiver as Shante spoke, "when I get to work I am going to look in the Accurient database and find every address he has ever used. He won't be hard to find. That database is better than the shit y'all use to run police checks!"

Listening to Shante had Asia wondering was her friend losing her mind. Never before had Shante reacted to a situation like this. With all the other pain that was brought into her life by her mother, someone would think she would plot like the Mendez brothers and take her mother out, but she didn't. All the years of cruelty and verbal abuse, her mother tormented her with it never pushed Shante over the edge. Thinking her friend was losing her mind, Asia slowly asked with a look of confusion on her face, "Have you stayed up this entire time?"

"I sure did! I popped me some No-Dose and me and Mary J was waiting on that ass!" Shante sounded as if what she did was okay and Asia shouldn't worry.

"Mary J? You had a gun?" Asia inquired.

"Naw girl. It was just me and I was playing my Mary J. Blige CD." Shante giggled.

"Well, Andre and 'em are moving my things today. I was going to work but if you need me to, I will take off and hang out with you today. I can tie up everything I need to before my wedding today." Asia watched as her chocolate drop exited the bathroom-dripping wet with a towel wrapped around his waist. She thought they would go another round when he came out but now that he had showered, she knew that was a sign that it wasn't going to happen because of him being late to do anything was definitely out the question.

"Asia, we can go hang out, but I don't want to do anything that has to do with a wedding. It's bad enough that in eight more days I will be standing next to you making a memorable moment knowing that my day won't be coming." Shante looked down at her engagement ring as she sat outside of Willie's apartment.

Asia looked around at the packed boxes. She thought this day was too cold to be moving, but she didn't give it another thought because she wouldn't be the one out in the cold. Before hanging up the phone Shante let Asia know, she did not have a problem driving. Asia hung up letting Shante know she would be ready within an hour.

As soon as Asia exited from the car, she remembered to call in. Shante drove over to Goody Goody restaurant. The entire time they were at Goody Goody attempting to eat breakfast, all Shante had to speak about was Willie. As they sat near the window in the diner, Shante watched every car that went by on Natural Bridge. Every Escalade that rode by caught her attention. Although Willie drove a black Escalade, Shante paid attention to everyone that passed.

After breakfast, the next thing on the agenda was the mall. The St. Louis Mills Mall was fairly new. The stay wasn't long because Asia thought that they might bump into the chic Willie was with or Willie himself. The next destination was the spa. It wasn't that far from the mall.

Asia signed her and Shante up for a full body massage, body wrap, facial, and pedicure. Shante entered the establishment feeling like that was long overdue. The soft sounds of smooth jazz filled the atmosphere. The vanilla aromatherapy was soothing to the nostrils. The hands of the masseur became so relaxing that Shante yearned for Willie's touch. She knew one spot she could find him, but she was in a battle of wondering did she really want to face him.

######

"Hello, Asia's residence." Andre held the phone. Glad it had ranged because he was ready to take a break from the great outdoors. It was too damn cold to be moving, but it needed to be done. It was his plan to get married on his father's birthday, February 17th. This day shared another special occasion; his parents were married on the same day thirty-six years ago.

Andre looked as his brother and his cousins as they poured in the door. He knew that once he stopped working they would wait for him. Andre appreciated the assistance. When he made mention of moving Asia's things, they just volunteered. He, his birth brother, and his cousins represented true brotherhood. Their fathers raised them that way.

Darryl, Darrell, Aaron, and Donald came in and took a break. They all popped open the caps on their Corona beers. Complaining about the weather, Aaron looked at his brother and said, "You and Asia better be together till death do y'all part. Got me moving all this shit in the dead of winter! You could have paid somebody to do this."

Andre's cousin Donald's freckles appeared to be jumping as he laughed gathering his words to speak, "Cuz has been with Asia for over ten years. I'm glad they're finally tying the knot."

Aaron looked at Donald. Aaron had to compare his love situation to Andre. He didn't take one eye off Donald as he spoke to him, "Crystal and I had been together since forever, had a baby together, and that bitch talking about it ain't going to work out because she got a girlfriend. So Donald, time doesn't mean shit to me!"

Everybody in the room shared a laugh. Aaron and Crystal had known each other since second grade. They all could remember the day that Crystal had given birth to Aaron's child. He was going to propose to her at the hospital so he asked everyone to come up to the hospital. Crystal informed Aaron that she was having this baby for her and her girlfriend right in front of Donald, Darryl, Darrell, Andre, Asia and Shante.

Andre decided it was time for him to cut the tension that was growing. He wore a proud grin as he stated, "I met that girl when she was in the tenth grade, my junior year of high school. When I went away to school in Jackson,

Mississippi, I thought I was going to find somebody older. If not that at least someone that reminded me of my mother. Those two years before I left, we became the best of friends. Asia knows my fears, my hopes, my wants, my desires, and my dreams. She knows me better than you!" He pointed to his brother Aaron, "shit she knows me betta than momma!" The sincerity and affection displayed in his eyes as she cried out.

The phone rang and Andre stepped in the kitchen to answer it. The caterer had called with some last minute arrangements. Andre looked around for something to write on. He grabbed a small notebook from the kitchen drawer. Flipping a couple of pages he found a blank sheet. He jotted down the few missing items along with the caterer's number and when the call ended, he rejoined his comrades.

Aaron was in search of his next beer. Aaron got up and headed to his kitchen in order to conquer his quest. He leaned on the counter, looked at his brother as he continued to brag about his lovely relationship with Asia, and drank from his bottle of beer.

Darrell, Donald, and Darryl continued to listen. Aaron grabbed the note pad, looked over the notes and began to flip through the pages. He looked over the names he found near the back of the notebook. He walked out of the kitchen area taking a swig of his beer as he placed the names in front of Andre, "Man, looks like you don't know all there is to know about Asia. She appears to have many miles on ha. She got her a hit list going."

Aaron didn't have anything against Asia. He adored her. His problem was his big brother's happiness. Aaron envied Andre so much. Andre was the first-born and Aaron always heard how he should be just like his big brother. Sometimes this interfered with his feelings. Andre never knew about Aaron's feelings of envy. It was evident it was there and everyone knew it but Andre.

Andre snatched the pad from Aaron's hand and took a good look at it. It was a list of names in Asia's handwriting. As Andre looked the list over, he could tell it was only males' names.

Donald look at the expression of disappointment on Andre's face, "You know the other day I was listening to the radio and they were talking about something similar to this. Somebody found a list where his fiancé had written down everybody she had sex with and they asked the question, "Would you wife her or kick that ass to the curb?"

Aaron looked down at the list and just named some names that weren't there. He began to recite an old *New Edition* song, "Ronnie, Bobbie, Rickey, and Mike. Looks like Asia got some miles on that ass!" Aaron began to laugh uncontrollably, "Wait a minute. I got a better one." Aaron placed his pointer finger up letting them know to hold on, "Now Dancer! Now Dasher! Now, Prancer and Vixen! Come, Cupid! Come, Comet; because Andre has to take Santa his ho ho!"

From the list of names, Aaron saw some familiar names. He recognized a few of his old classmates. He knew that Andre was upset but he wouldn't dare look at him. He wanted Andre brought back to his reality and feel the pain he once felt. Being the younger brother who couldn't live up to, a standard that was set so high sometime interfered with Aaron's better judgment.

Donald looked at Aaron and next turning toward

Andre, "Man that might not be what that list means. You should ask her about that before you jump to some crazy conclusions. Aaron you need to cut that shit out." Donald knew Aaron was trying to push Andre over the edge.

With eyes fiery red and holding back his tears he yelled, "Go get all that shit off that truck!" He was caught up in his emotions. Asia had caused him some embarrassment in front of the last people he wanted to be embarrassed in front of. To them he always came out on top and that's how he liked it. He wanted to compare his life next to perfect.

The very moment when the truck was unloaded, everyone left. Andre stayed because he needed to address this situation with Asia face-to-face. He didn't know if he was going to beat her or kill her the second she walked through that front door. He sat staring at the door holding the notebook. He was trying to gain some understanding from the list. Although he only waited for forty-five minutes, it seemed like five hours. Within those forty-five minutes, he had a photocopy of every single one of the names in his personal memory book. He went from staring at the door to staring at the notebook. When he heard a noise from horns blowing outside to car doors slamming he thought it was Asia. Once he realized Asia hadn't shown up, he looked back at the notebook as if he were studying the names.

Asia walked through the door. She looked directly into Andre's eyes. In all the years, she had known him she hadn't seen this look since his basketball team didn't win the state championship during his junior year of high school. She looked at his hands as he handed her the notebook. Asia looked at the names she had written four days ago when she and Shante were strolling down memory lane. The night Shante came over they discussed what took place on the radio show. It enticed her to write down the names on her hit list. The very list Andre was holding in his hands.

"Tell me what this is supposed to mean." He watched her movement trying to make a judgment from her reactions, "I think we need to go get tested first thing tomorrow. We can go right to the health department."

Asia couldn't say a word. She was thinking of something to say but her mouth would not let one word escape. She was wishing that she could drastically change this circumstance. She tried to look him in his face but her eyes looked right pass him. She was finding it very difficult to give him any eye contact. For years of longing for acceptance and love, she was now experiencing some guilt.

He looked at Asia as if she were yesterday's trash. The list was leaving a very nasty taste in his mouth. Andre articulated every word slowly while walking out of the apartment and slamming the door so hard the entire apartment shook. "Asia, you are WASHED UP!"

Asia looked down at the list that she made with Shante after listening to the radio segment while on her way home from having her hair braided. Asia thought about the segment long and hard. It made her realize she was in a similar situation so she counted everybody that had entered her soul. Together she and Shante reminisced and Shante told her not to write it down because it may fall in the wrong hands. It had done just that.

Asia and Andre knew everything that there was to know about one another. Asia knew Andre better than his very own mother. Now Andre knew something that Asia never planned to let him know.

Asia was left with the feeling of rejection. This was a feeling that Asia had grown immune. One day with no explanation at all, Asia was dropped off at her Uncle Rob's. Robert was Asia's mother Janice's older and only brother.

Asia tried so hard to erase her mother from her memory and it wasn't hard. The minute Andre slammed the door those memories of her mother began to surface. She balled herself up in a fetal position holding her knees close to her chest. The feeling of wanted to be loved had resurfaced. She needed someone to comfort her.

Asia could remember the incident vividly as if it happened to her yesterday. She walked into her mother's bedroom of their two-bedroom apartment and found her mother crying unbearably. This was nothing unusual because the last two weeks she found her mother knelt down beside her bed with a face flushed with tears.

######

Janice, Asia's mother, had seemed always to have a tough time. Janice's mother died when she was nine and she and her brother, Robert, were placed in foster care. Robert was eight years older than Janice was. At seventeen, he only had one year left in foster care. A year that became lucky for him.

He was placed with a family who had raised six boys. He would beg his foster mother to get his sister, but she didn't want to bring a young girl around a place where all kinds of men went in and out the door.

Robert's foster family had a family business and owned

a couple of apartment buildings. The foster care was for legitimate reasons only. His foster family's close relative was the director of the program and a part of the family business.

Janice finally found some stability when she reached eighteen. She was able to stay with Robert and his girlfriend, Wanda, who eventually became his wife. In the beginning, Wanda and Janice got along very fine. Then all of a sudden, the situation changed. Janice would be sitting near Robert at either dinner or just watching the television, she would whisper in his ear and they would look at Wanda and laugh. Then Janice started lying on Wanda. Whatever Janice would say, Robert would believe her and react toward Wanda. Janice didn't have very many friends but everyone that she brought to the house she was trying to hook up with her brother. Wanda paid attention to this all, but she was too afraid to say a word. She and Robert lived the good life until Janice came in and interrupted it all. During all the mischief Janice was causing, she managed to find her someone.

When Robert first came around his foster family, they had high traffic. After a while, there was a minimal amount of traffic coming and going. Shortly after Janice moved in it seemed as though the traffic had picked back up. That's when Janice met Asia's father. Anthony was a longtime friend of Robert's foster family. He was about to have a career in the military.

Anthony had joined the army. He was doing a tour of duty over in Asia. Janice had so many pictures of him and his platoon in their Army fatigue holding their weapons in some Asian village. Janice could remember all the names of the places he was stationed. He had been to Bangladesh, Philippines, Hong Kong, and Taiwan.

On the day Asia was born, all the lies began to unfold.

He promised Janice he would be there for the birth of his child. That was his plan but it didn't quite happen that way. He told her that he was released on an honorable discharge but what he really meant was he had gone absent without official leave.

Anthony's first day back in the states was very chaotic. He survived the shooting and was able to leave the scene of the crime. He was feeling like this day was his lucky day. He survived a minor gunshot wound and walked away with a couple of hundred dollars. His luck soon ran short. When he made it to a place where he thought he could get some help, he realized the place was being robbed by a bunch of off duty cops that refused to leave any witnesses to identify them.

Janice sat up in her hospital bed gazing out of the window. The sounds of wheels clicking as hospital beds moved through the hall and voices coming over the intercom system were faded in her background. The scent of strong medicines had her drifting about in her thoughts. She was wondering why Anthony had not made it to the hospital. The flashing of a star caught her attention. She held on to her newborn baby tightly. Janice ignored all that was taking place around her.

She could remember Anthony telling her, "Whenever you get lonely look to the sky because in times of darkness a star will shine to let you know that I am there for you. That star represents how we will always have each other. Our love will be represented by all the shining stars above."

That's why Janice was on her knees. She looked out the window and saw the star shining so bright. It was five years ago on this very day that the love of her life had been murdered. Every day she looked into Asia's face, she could see Anthony.

The man who was the father of her child never got a chance to see his daughter.

On the anniversary of Anthony's death is when she decided she was no longer to be fit to be a single mother. Her brother was giving a woman something she wanted to give her daughter, a family. Janice felt like Robert and Wanda would be the best place for Asia.

Janice drove in her green Nova not saying one word to her daughter. Asia could remember going to Uncle Rob's house on holidays but her mother never left her there. They sat in front of Uncle Rob's house. Janice looked down at her daughter. All she could see was Anthony. She looked at her daughter the way Anthony looked at her and spoke, "Whenever you get lonely; I want you to look to the sky and find the brightest star. That star will let you know that I am always with you."

Asia didn't understand one word that her mother was saying. It had her very confused. When they arrived at Robert's house her mother instructed her to go knock on the door to see if anyone was there, Asia did what she was instructed to do not knowing what would happen next.

As the door opened, Asia turned to look back and Janice's face was filled with tears as she waved at her child. Asia was looking more confused than she was before she got out the car. She had no idea that was going to be the last time she would ever see her mother.

Asia walked into the house. Wanda was preparing dinner. After dinner, Asia stood in the window. Months had gone past before she realized her mother wasn't coming back.

Chapter 5

WHAT'S DONE IN THE DARK

Trying to keep his thoughts going anywhere near Asia, he started his day by going through several reports he allowed to pile up on his desk. His goal for today was to keep his mind off Asia and make sure that not one detail was missing in any of his reports. Andre worked as a plainclothes detective. He spent majority of his time investigating, gathering facts and collecting evidence for criminal cases. Majority of his assignments were interagency task forces to combat specific types of crime. He had his hand in conducting interviews, examining records, observing the activities of suspects, and participating in drug raids or arrests.

His current case involved intimidation. The sister of a suspect in a domestic situation allegedly threatened the suspect's girlfriend. The arraignment wasn't until 1 p.m. and he had five hours of trying to keep himself occupied doing something. He never knew how his day would start or how his day would end. Today he just knew what he didn't want to take place.

Andre had worked his way up the ranks in the city of St. Louis, Missouri Metropolitan Police Department. It wasn't long after he had completed the police academy that he went from working as a police officer for the eighth district to being promoted to a detective of the same district. Many believed it had a lot to do with the fact of his father being the Deputy

Chief of Criminal Investigations. He was not ready to take on another job duty because of the hassles that came when he made the accomplishment of becoming a detective. Andre had a brother and a few cousins on the force longer than him. This alone had many of the officers speculating his status within the department. Most believed his family members should have gotten some promotions since they had been there longer.

Andre and Aaron's father had that Joe Jackson mentality. He solely believed that you had to work hard for what you want. Aaron was not to do anything that involved a difficult task. In all the speculations that were taken place with Andre becoming a detective, no one took into consideration that he possessed a Bachelor's Degree in Criminal Justice and plus he passed the test.

Detective Robinson walked over to the narrow office space of Detective Townsend. Robinson noticed something about his partner's demeanor. Andre's partner had fifteen years of seniority over Andre. Robinson held Andre's best interest but Robinson sometimes displayed a slight envious manner. Andre paid it no mind. Robinson would joke about how his body looked sometime ago. Andre tried to look beyond the pop belly Robinson had.

Andre could see Robinson coming near his cubicle. Robinson moved swiftly toward him. He wore his deep gray suit nicely. The color gray made his gray eyes stand out more and complimented in his yellow skin tone. Andre laughed to himself thinking about how Robinson would always say light skin was on the comeback.

Robinson had been married to his high school sweetheart for the past thirty-three years. He knew the look of woman problems instantly. He had seen many in his day. He was thinking about how he was going to approach Andre because he knew the last thing he wanted to do was discuss the real problem.

"What time is the arraignment?" Robinson rubbed his baldhead waiting on a response.

"It's not till one." Andre never looked up. He was looking at his paper work as though he was studying for an exam.

Robinson was really trying to figure out of all the cases to deal with, why Andre wanted to waste his time dealing with some domestic violence threat. He wanted to make a joke about Andre threatening Asia and what would happen if the state picked charges up against him. He chose otherwise because whatever was taking place he knew it involved Asia, so he refrained from even saying her name.

"Have you eaten breakfast?" Robinson wasn't even about to wait on an answer. He was about to get Andre away from the desk anyway he could.

Andre wanted to sit and mope but he decided against it. He grabbed his jacket from the back of his chair. Robinson turned to walk away and Andre followed behind. Right as they pulled from out the police station's parking lot, the dispatcher came over the radio.

The dispatcher announced a homicide case. A homeless man had called in to identify a corpse wrapped in a black plastic bag. Robinson waited to hear the location announced once again. The car was now headed to the downtown area toward the riverfront.

The arch grounds were flooded with police. Several officers were questioning the homeless man. The entire scene had been taped off and the crime unit was pulling up the same time Andre and Robinson pulled up. Walking toward the crime scene, right on the arch grounds, Andre could see the black plastic bag. He and Robinson walked over to the corpse. A male uniformed officer unzipped the plastic showing the detectives the face of the victim.

Andre looked down, over his years with the department; this was the first time that a corpse made him tremble. When he noticed the small black mole under the victims left eye, he got dizzy. Andre quickly turned as he began to vomit. Robinson knew he wasn't having a good day. Before he could make it to the side of his partner and offer any assistance, Andre had collapsed.

"Zip her back up and get her out of here!" Robinson yelled, "Someone call the paramedics!"

######

"Congratulations baby!" Asia wrapped her hands around Andre's neck and landed a sloppy kiss directly on his lips.

Andre held on to her tightly. He was so happy. Graduation was finally here.

"Way to go Dre!" one of his teammates from basketball smiled as he passed by the two.

"My boy!" the dude that played center from the football team walked up, shook his hand, and embraced him before he walked away.

Asia stood by his side as he waited for his parents to meet up with them. After the graduation, they all were going to dinner. Asia smiled as everyone walked over to get a picture of Andre. Most of the females gave Asia a fake smile as others motioned her to join in the picture. Asia didn't care what no one else was doing. She knew right then that Andre loved no one but her. The night had ended and before Asia knew it, Andre was packing up to leave for Jackson, Mississippi.

Andre was housed in the Alexander Hall. His roommate, Melvin, was from Memphis, Tennessee. Most of the roommates were paired according to their majors. Melvin and Andre shared the same major, but the two guys next door, Jake and Tyrone, had two very different majors. Andre was cool with Melvin. Through the years, they spent a whole a lot of time getting to know one another.

Melvin stood six feet tall and had that Mos Def swagger. His skin tone was dark chocolate with enormous eyes. His hair was dreadful. The locks appeared to be filthy and matted. Melvin's hair was the only problem that Andre had with him. When Andre greeted him, he thought to himself that they were going to make a bet that Melvin would lose. The consequences for the loser would be a haircut.

Jake and Tyrone was the black version of dumb and dumber. Those two had just met when they reached the dorm. Jake was from Biloxi, Mississippi and had a southern tang that made you think he was born in the 1920's. He was very polite; he constantly said, "No sir" and "yes sir" when he was engaged in a conversation. Jake possessed that Hershey's dark chocolate complexion and some slender kissable lips. He wore a precise trimmed blended fade.

Tyrone was from Grenada, Mississippi. As fine as he was, most females ignored how dim-witted he was. Tyrone was well done, with skin as smooth as a baby's ass. He had a low afro, which was tapered, to his beard line. He could have very well passed as Morris Chestnut's son.

Andre, Melvin, Jake and Tyrone hit it off from the start. They were all into to the sports and all had been quarterbacks during their high school years. Andre and Tyrone were the only two to play both football and basketball. Tyrone was even on the wrestling team.

Majority of their classes were together. Sometimes they would take turns going to class while the other chilled in the dorm. They did their homework assignments together as well as studied for their midterms together. The first semester was a breeze as they were each other's support system. Andre and

Melvin soon came to realize that Jake and Tyrone was no dummy when it came to the books. They just lacked common sense. By the second semester, they had college life figured out. They hooked up with some freshman girls that were in their classes and basically had them doing all their work. This was Andre's first mistake.

When he first reached Jackson, Mississippi, he did have intentions on finding the companion of a female to settle down with. He even thought about finding someone that was goal oriented that he could wife. Now, he loved Asia dearly but he did have a slight problem with her future choices. He knew Asia once spoke of becoming a fashion designer, but she did not know what fashion she wanted to design. He had seen her sketch a few designs, but she didn't appear to be pursuing the dream. The only ups she had on the fashion were being familiar with the latest designs.

Andre was happy that she lived her dreams through him but he wanted someone who was headstrong and took charge of her own life. That's what connected him to Regina. She knew what she wanted and he really admired that in her. In their American Government Survey course, Regina would stand toe to toe with the professor. Everything he said she would challenge it. Her plans were to become a prosecuting attorney. She had the ultimate goal of becoming the first black female United States Attorney General.

"Ms. Washington, do you mind if I address you as Regina?" the professor asked as he looked into some very confident eyes.

Regina positioned her small petite frame in her seat. Her hair was pulled back into a ponytail and she rubbed both sides of her head. She looked over the top of her framed Chanel eyeglasses. Andre thought that the small black mole under her left eye was very sexy. She sat in her desk showing off her perfect set of pearly whites, "If you don't mind me addressing you as Hubert." Regina smoothed her hand over her slender lips and the class began to chuckle.

The Professor smiled at her as if he was admiring her beauty. He had a soft spot in his heart for her because she was the only one in his class that appeared to be there to learn. She reminded him of his boisterous wife. He looked directly at her as he cleared his throat, loosened up his tie and looked over the top of his eyeglasses, "Ms. Washington, what is your career choice?"

Regina took a look at her classmates. She wanted to make sure she had everyone's undivided attention. Andre was waiting to hear what she had to say. Her attitude put a completely new meaning to, "I'm bossy." Regina placed her hands together. "I plan to become the top prosecuting attorney throughout the United States and eventually gain the attention of the President so that he can appoint me as the first black female United States Attorney General."

The professor glanced around the room, "Bill Clinton put the first women in that seat already."

"When did Janet Reno become black?" Regina looked at him as if he were stupid. Right as he was about to address the topic, the classes abruptly got up out of their seats. Everyone but the professor and Regina was paying attention to the time.

Andre approached his future homework buddy as soon as the class was over. From that day on, he and Regina became the best of friends. Regina was from St. Louis also, she graduated from Cardinal Ritter as Valedictorian. Cardinal Ritter was a Catholic high school located in North St. Louis City. It served as an educational program that prepared its students for leadership roles in a multi-ethnic society.

Andre couldn't believe that they were from the same city. With her attending Cardinal Ritter, they hung out with two totally different groups of people. He wouldn't have seen her at any games because they would have only played Cardinal Ritter in some statewide championship games. The moment Andre spoke to Regina he didn't know he had her.

Regina grew up in a household of six brothers. She was the youngest and the only girl. She had been the baby in the Washington's household for last ten years. After six boys, she was her father's pride and joy. She learned to play rough and do most handy things like putting up drywall, laying carpet, and odd plumbing jobs. When her dad saw her so into her books, that's what he flourished her with.

Mr. Washington was originally from Jackson, Mississippi. When he visited his mother's sister in St. Louis, he adapted to the city life and didn't leave. Regina would become intrigued by the story of how her aunt married a Caucasian man. During the time Regina's aunt married this man, St. Louis was very unfriendly. The city was so unfriendly that her great aunt's murder went unsolved. She and her husband were burned beyond recognition in their two-story home. Regina's father inherited their family business.

Mr. Washington owned his own construction company and each of Regina's brothers worked for the company. Regina's mother was a registered nurse. Her parents met when her mother was doing a student intern at an area hospital and her father came in to get his foot bandaged due to a heavy piece of a steel beam falling on his foot. On this particular day, he was not wearing any steel toe boots. He had only fractured his big toe. So he got an ace bandage, a phone number and was on his merely way. A few months later they married and they been together ever since. Together they strived for the best for their children. For Regina, accomplishing nothing but the best was programmed and manufactured in her from day one.

Melvin's head was representing the Rastafarian movement as he wore a yellow and green knitted hat. He walked into the dorm room, "What are you about to get into today?" As he shut the door, he sat at the desk that was on the opposite of the room from the beds. The desk sat between the two closets. They had moved the desk from between the beds so the desk lamp wouldn't shine in the face of whoever was sleeping.

Andre lay on his stomach with his head deep in his *Philosophy for Logical Thinking* textbook. He stopped his studying to respond to Melvin. Before he could answer, he noticed Jake and Tyrone making themselves comfortable. Jake stood over him and Tyrone took a seat on Melvin's bed. Andre rose up so that Jake wouldn't be standing over his head.

Andre looked over at Tyrone, "As hot as it is why the hell you got on all black? You look like you about to rob some damn body."

Tyrone let a smirk come across his face, "You were breaking grounds and taking charge last night. You are definitely the robber out of this bunch."

Jake gave Tyrone some dap. He walked over to Andre and softly punched him in his arm. Jake grabbed a seat right next to him as all the boys shared a laugh.

Melvin leaned back in his chair, "This dude got a girl back home and a girl here at school." He looked at Andre, "What's going to happen when you two get back to the Lou and Regina wants to hook up with you. How are you gonna swing that?"

Andre looked around the room and his friends waited on an answer, "That's one bridge I will worry about crossing when I get to it!"

Melvin threw Andre a notebook, "I want you to write down all the little chicken heads that you have ran through since you been here for the last two years."

Andre threw the notebook right back at him, "You write that mess down. I truly live by the motto no evidence, no witnesses, not guilty."

Tyrone chuckled, "DNA tops all that!"

Andre stood up, "DNA ain't got anything to do with this!"

Regina knocked then entered the room.

Melvin turned his head to the direction of the door, "Well damn come on in!"

Regina walked in and Andre looked her over. She was looking rather different. She didn't have on any glasses and her hair was not pulled back into a ponytail. It was hanging to her shoulders and her bangs lay softly on her forehead emphasizing a sexy look within her eyes. The bangs were flipped in the infamous Farrah Fawcett hairstyle.

She was not dressed in her usual jeans or jogging suit. She was wearing a wide neck fuchsia shirt-dress with some black sexy shoes that laced up her legs. Andre stood up, put on his white T-shirt, and grabbed his red Cardinal fitted baseball cap.

Melvin watched his roommate as he was about to walk out the door, "We can't go?"

"We are about to drive for a couple of hours to a casino." Andre looked back at Melvin. Melvin didn't need to ask whose car because he knew that majority of Regina's family was in Jackson and she probably had one of her relative's cars.

Melvin stood up, "The casino is the safest place to be. They got security and cameras. The eye in the sky watches it all. Some fool trip up in a casino if he wants to, mother fuckers will come out from everywhere swarming the spot like bees on honey."

Regina looked back wanting to taunt their emotions, "You all are welcomed to come along, only if Melvin shaves his head."

Melvin looked over at Regina. He was flipping through his mental catalogue to come up with some positive words to regurgitate. He smiled, "Enjoy and I will catch you all when you get back."

Regina stood with her hand on her side, the sway of neck and the bucking of her eyes, the following words slide off her tongue, "I thought you were going to choose to stay behind because I know you were not about to get smart with the driver." She dangled the car keys. No one needed to be asked a second time. They all left the dorm room and headed to the car. Regina had one of her cousin's vehicles.

Regina chirped the alarm and the doors unlocked. Melvin looked over to where she was walking and where he thought he heard the beeping sound coming from. Melvin grabbed Andre by the arm, "Are you sure this is her cousin's car? This could be some dude's car."

The two of them laughed as they entered a tricked out four door 1998 purple Chevrolet Caprice Classic. The twenty-two inch DUB chrome rims and tires looked like they didn't fit the car. The fact that five people would be in the car would go unnoticed because of the tinted windows.

They all took their places in the car. Regina revved the engine and pulled off the parking lot. She looked in the rearview mirror into Melvin's face, "I bet you are going to cut those snakes of your head before we leave JSU."

Melvin laughed, "Quit tripping off my head. I am like Samson; my strength is in my hair." He tightened his fist as he raised his arms and began to flex his muscles.

Jake smacked his arm down because he had elbowed him all up in his chin. He twirled his head, "Dude, watch what the hell you doing!"

Regina didn't mind the company. For the past two years, she had gotten very use to all of them hanging out together. She didn't like the fact that if they were going to an off-campus party, she wasn't invited and if she really wanted to go, Andre would stay back.

Andre woke up. He hadn't talk to his father in a while. No one had called him and neither did he attempt to call anybody. He had talked to Asia a couple of times. She was making sure that he didn't need anything. Since he decided to stay in Jackson over the holidays, she wanted to make sure he was doing fine and if he needed anything, she was going to take care of it.

Andre sat listening to the phone ring. Finally, there was an answer.

"What's up little brother?" Andre spoke with excitement. He was glad that someone was there to take the call.

"Nothing! What's up with you?" Aaron already made up in his mind that he was not about to be on the phone long.

"I ain't doing nothing but modulating." Andre laughed. "I can't wait till I get done with school. I miss being around Asia." He just slid that in to cover up the fact that he considered them having an open relationship. He simply blamed it on the distance.

"She ain't up to nothing. She will be waiting on you when you get back. Her and Shante walking around this place like they thicker than thieves. What you need to be is getting Asia to hook me up with Shante."

Andre chuckled. He knew that although he loved his brother and he knew his brother loved him, a slight bit of envy filled his body. Aaron has always had to play the background and Andre knew Aaron didn't like him being in the spotlight.

"How are you doing down there with the sports and stuff, Dre?"

"I ain't doing nothing. I haven't tried out for anything since my freshman year. These coaches ain't doing nothing but sleeping on my talents. I was treated like a second-class citizen when I tried out for the football team and the basketball team. They missed the memo about Andre Townsend. They didn't know I was the man in my city."

"Sounds like you WASHED UP down in those parts." Aaron was glad to hear that. He never tried out for anything because he feared people would tell him he was nothing like his brother and he had grown tired of it hearing that from his parents all of his life. Aaron filled Andre in on his mother and the latest happenings that were going on with their father. He continued talking about their cousins. Although Aaron had a slight jealous problem with his brother, he still loved him. When Andre suggested that they get off the phone, Aaron was not ready to bring the conversation to an end. Andre let him know when he would be calling back and they hung up the phone. Aaron didn't know why he told him when he would be calling because if he needed to talk to him he wasn't going to announce anything.

Andre was preparing to come home for summer break. He had a week before finals and two weeks before he would pack up and go home for his summer break. He would get down with a few chicks here and there. He limited himself once he and Regina made a close connection. Through it all, no one could replace Asia. She had looked out for him when he had started having financial problems. Although she was a hundred miles away, he missed her. He missed the way her heart shaped lips would pucker to kiss him. He decided that instead of laying there thinking of her he would give her a call. He tried calling Asia but he didn't receive an answer. As he was about to call her back, he could hear a lot of commotion coming from outside of his dorm room window.

Melvin bust through the door, "Dre, you need to get outside! Regina has passed out or something."

Andre didn't even hang the phone up. He followed Melvin outside to the entrance area of Alexandria Hall. About thirty yards from the door, he could see someone laid out in the grass.

Asia tried to call Andre back only to a busy signal. She was wondering why he hadn't left a message. She tried several times to contact him. She suddenly remembered that before he had phone in his room he would use a pay phone. She could call the pay phone at anytime.

Asia made the call to the pay phone. Frantically, someone eventually answered the phone. Asia was alarmed in the way the person had answered the phone. She hesitantly began to speak, "Hello, may I speak to Andre?"

"He not here!" That's all Asia heard before the telephone receiver was slammed. Asia just decided to wait for

Andre to call her back.

Just as the paramedics arrived on the scene, Andre had made it over to the grassy area. When he noticed the small black mole under Regina's left eye he got dizzy. She looked to be in a comatose state.

The paramedics pulled out their defibrillator. The police made the crowd step back. Andre was allowed to be the closest one in the area after he disclosed that he was her next of kin.

"One, two, three, clear!" The female paramedic used the defibrillator machine to shock the heart. She was attempting to return Regina's heart back into a regular beating pattern. After several attempts, there was a sign of a heartbeat. Regina's heartbeat was very low and her pulse was weak.

The paramedics moved about quickly placing Regina on the stretcher and immediately placing her in the ambulance. The sirens were turned on and the ambulance sped off. One of the staff members from the dorm rode in the ambulance.

Andre went ballistic. Melvin stood by his friend's side. He could see the hurt as Andre began to fight the air. Melvin walked up to him and embraced him. Andre embraced him back as he began to cry a river.

Melvin began to wipe away Andre's tears, "Dre, pull yourself together so that we can go check on Regina. Everything is going to be okay."

Andre looked at his friend in such a short time they had become very tight. He took a deep breath. He leaned down placing his hands on his knees as he stood on his feet. The center of his back rose continuously as he took several deep breaths. Andre didn't know what to do. He heard Melvin as he spoke, but he couldn't understand why he wasn't allowed to ride with Regina. He thought he had lost her but when Melvin mentioned going to the hospital he realized that there was still some hope after all.

Regina never mentioned any of her health problems. Ever since she was very young, she has had complications from blood clots. Once she and Andre became sexually active, she began to take birth control pills. When she began to take the pills, she was instructed by her doctor to stop. Due to her medical condition, she would experience an overwhelming amount of blood clotting. Although blood clotting is a natural process, the birth control would make the clotting worse. Several blood clots formed which blocked a few arteries in Regina's heart. Her heart was not able to pump enough blood. Regina died from congestive heart failure as soon as the ambulance got her to the hospital.

Being that all of Regina's family was right in Jackson, all the arrangements were made there. A week after she had lay in the grass, she was now laying in her final resting place. Andre was sitting near the front of the church. He was in such a deep trans, he didn't hear the church bell ring three times as the time was eleven clock on the dot. He sat on the second pew with the casket in perfect view. He wasn't paying attention to the traffic that was coming and going. Her visitation had been set from ten to twelve. The funeral service was scheduled to start immediately following the visitation.

The atmosphere was calm and a small amount of whispering could be heard. Andre ignored it all. His name was called and he didn't answer until he felt a tap on his shoulder. He looked up and noticed that Melvin was looking like Michael

Jordan by the head. The Rastafarian movement was over for him. Regina told him he was going to cut his hair before he left Jackson State University. Andre and Melvin both were thinking about what Regina said. As Melvin glanced at Andre, together they both shared a laugh.

Asia had finally caught up with Andre. It had been nine whole days since he last tried to contact her and she hadn't heard from him. Andre was staring at his ceiling in deep thoughts. The phone had ranged about eight times before he realized it was ringing.

With the driest voice ever, he answered the phone, "This, Dre."

"Hello Mr. M.I.A!"

The very moment he heard Asia's voice he rose up coming out of his slump as though she could see him. "Hey baby."

"Damn you call me and I call you back and the line stayed busy. Then I call the payphone at the dorm and some rude individual didn't even take the time out to ask me my name. They slammed the damn phone down as if he ain't here and you are bothering me. I was shocked because that never happened before. To put the icing on the cake it's been nine whole days."

Andre didn't want to hear anymore. She had never been the type to nag and he sure didn't want her to start. Today wasn't going to be the day he started allowing her to nag. "Asia slow your roll. Girl a lot has happened. The day I called you, one of my classmates died. It was so frantic. The whole campus was crying. People were hugging each other and trying to console each other. That was a very sad day for us here." Andre was trying not to think about Regina, as he talked with Asia afraid that he might call her the wrong name.

"Oh baby I am so sorry to hear that. What happened to

him?"

"It was a female and she died of congestive heart failure." Andre began to wish very hard that that would go right over her head. With a moment of silence, he thought it did.

"Andre, hold the fuck up," she paused because she actually had to think about her very own infidelity that was taking place while he was away, "some female and it took me nine days to catch up with you. What you and this girl were getting down or something?"

"Look Asia, it's nothing like that. You know my mother is sick and all about my financial problems. I was thinking about not coming home and getting a summer job to pay for all this. The only thing is it might take me longer to graduate."

"Well baby, let me know what you need. I will help you out whenever I can. I hate that you are thinking about not coming home for the summer. I really miss you."

"I am going to go head and get off this phone. I talk to you later." Andre was about to get back into the little slump he had been in every since Regina's death nine days ago.

"Alright baby. I love you." Asia grinned.

"Asia, I love you, too."

Asia looked out for Andre during that summer he didn't come home. He didn't even have to work the summer as he had planned. She was doing so good making sure he had some funds he took a summer course that Asia didn't know that she financed.

######

Almost thirty minutes had passed before Andre came to. The little girl was a twelve-year-old runaway. She had been missing for two months. There were posters placed all over the city. Runaways weren't something that Andre dealt with on a regular basis. He saw the picture but never really paid it any mind.

Robinson placed his hand on his pop belly, "Is there anything you want to talk about?" He stood holding the passenger side door staring into Andre's eyes. They had been partners for a very long time and he never saw Andre so weak.

"That young girl reminded me of someone I dated in college and I never told Asia about it. Right now, we have a very complicated situation-taking place that I wish not to share. Furthermore, I rather not even talk about this." Andre rested his head back on the headrest of the car.

Chapter 6

BRANDON

"Have you ever had your pussy ate?" Brandon gave Asia a smile waiting on her response. He was hoping that she said no. Most high school scholars weren't quite on his sexual level just yet. Brandon was before his time. He could thank his big brother, Harold, for that. He was twelve years his senior and the Don Juan with the debonair attitude in their household.

Asia walked down the stairway of Deaconess Hospital. She looked to the left at the elderly Caucasian couple with salt and pepper hair to see if by any chance they had overheard the hideous words that had just exited Brandon's oral cavity.

Asia's caramel complexion turned scarlet red as she partially grew a kool-aid smile from the slight hint of embarrassment and a rush full of anticipation for the act in which he had proposed.

Brandon watched the slender legs glide down the stairway. The short boy cut blue jean shorts she wore made Asia legs appear to be longer than they actually were. The five-foot frame looked to be five foot five.

Brandon waited on Asia to catch up. When she made it to the sidewalk, he placed a kiss on her check and grabbed her Gucci link gold chain, "By the time I get through with you, you going to let me rock this!"

Asia rolled her eyes with a devilish grin. It wasn't her

chain to pass off, in the first place.

The visit of Brandon's newborn niece was short and the ride back to his bungalow in the basement of his mother's house was even shorter.

Asia lay looking in the ceiling while Brandon had buried his head in her treasure box. He nibbled, sucked, and chewed as if he were a child playing with his pacifier. Periodically, Asia could feel the sharpness of his teeth. Being that this was her first time, she didn't know whether this experience should have been a pleasurable one or a painful one.

No sounds of intimacy could be heard. It was as if someone had pushed mute. The silence abruptly came to an end once Brandon had placed all of his manhood inside. The squeaking of the lifeless mattress bearing no headboard could be heard for miles. Brandon was nothing like Andre. Andre had been the first to enter and this was nothing like her first time. She laid there trying to figure out how she had ended up in Brandon's bed in the first place.

Andre, Asia, Shante and Brandon all attended Beaumont Senior High School. Brandon knew very well that the All-American senior, Andre, was dating the sophomore that everyone wanted. Brandon figured it was fair game. He had one year remaining to be with Asia so he was opening that door to some type of opportunity. Asia welcomed Brandon with open arms.

Asia walked with confidence. She dressed in the latest fashions. Her style was overall unique. Although she wore, what everyone else was wearing, the way she put it together made a bold statement. While others dressed down, she dressed up everything. Her clothing was neatly pressed. Her belt, shoes, and purses coincided with her attire. Her hair was never out of place. The bob that she wore was trimmed neatly. She didn't over do it with her jewelry. Most girls were into tennis shoes she had a few pair, but tennis usually was not her typical choice of shoe. Asia went for more of the casual shoes designed by Cole Haan, Etienne Aigner, Franco Sarto, and Kenneth Cole. She felt these were more of her caliber. Shante's attire was very similar to Asia's.

"Excuse me, Asia, could you pass me the chocolate milk."

Asia grabbed the milk before looking at the figure that asked for the milk, which stood behind her in the lunch line. As she turned to hand the patron what he asked for, she quickly sized him up. Asia smiled at the chubby fellow. His weight worked in his favor. It added to his swagger. He was clean cut with a low fade and his complexion was almost the same color of his khaki pants. His Colgate smile turned Asia on.

"Here you go." Asia handed him the small carton of milk.

"Brandon." He smiled, looking like a brighter shade of Cedric the Entertainer.

"What is the name dropping for?" Asia queried.

"I know you wanted to ask, therefore, being the generous person that I am, I told you my name." Brandon showed off his pearly whites.

Asia caught up with Shante in their usual corner seats in the back of the school cafeteria where they could see all the activity that went on. Shante and Asia were two of a kind. They would socialize here and there with some of their classmates, but they had a very special bond.

Brandon sat in clear view of Asia. He would wave at her periodically followed up with a wink and Asia would show off her dimples with a phony grin. Before the week had ended, Brandon had her number and a date on Friday night.

"Asia! Girl, somebody is at the door for you!" Uncle Rob yelled toward the back of the apartment, as he made his way back into his gray worn out recliner.

Asia walked toward the front of the apartment, which she shared, with her aunt Wanda, her uncle, and two cousins, Keith and Tyrone. Keith and Tyrone were average little boys. You could find them throwing rocks, flipping on dirty mattresses or doing something uncanny. One-day things changed for them. They had drunk a substance that was concocted just for them. It didn't kill them but it left them walking around like zombies.

Uncle Rob figured this sudden change was due to the fact that the majority of Wanda's family showed mental issues and it had caught up with his boys. Robert was raised that doctors were only needed when something severe happened. Had he taken his boys to the doctor, he would have found out that a mixture of heroin, whiskey, had poisoned them along with a finely ground, gray-black powder phosphate used in rat poison that affected the central nervous system. Had it been more potent with phosphate they would have both died.

Asia rolled her eyes at her bubble-eyed uncle. She loved him dearly for taking her in when her mother decided motherhood wasn't for her and ran off. She just hated the fact that every now and then, he would say cruel things to his wife and before his sons became delusional, they would help in the taunting and teasing of their mother.

Brandon came in to meet the family. He sized up Wanda. He didn't know what to say. It only appeared to him that he needed to start watching his weight because the reality of being obese was starring him in the face. Wanda's cheeks were so massive that you couldn't see that her beauty was beyond skin deep.

Uncle Rob, Keith, and Tyrone were just as slim as Jimmie Walker was, when he ran around in Good Times yelling "Dy-No-Mite!" With the three gentlemen being three shades of brown only, distinguish their identities. Robert definitely possessed some strong genes. At thirteen, Tyrone stood as tall as his sixteen-year-old brother did. Both boys were almost two inches shy of their father's height.

Uncle Rob was a grease monkey. He and Keith nearly resembled, complexion wise. Robert worked mostly in back alleys and part-time at the tire shop his friend owned. Asia's state assistance got them through, Wanda's food stamps kept them fed, and being that Robert's comrade and boss from the tire shop owned the apartment building in which they resided, no one wanted for anything.

Andre was away at school and Brandon was Asia's breath of fresh air. Brandon had dropped out of school in order to pursue other things. With him being away from school, their relationship went unnoticed by most. On occasions, a few classmates would see them hanging out. When Brandon bought himself a car, he felt the need to pick-up Asia so she wouldn't have to ride the bus home. Shante was there for the ride and majority of the time Brandon had a passenger so she and Asia would hop in the back seat together. Asia didn't need Aaron telling his brother anything.

Fall ended and winter hit. The time Brandon was spending with Asia minimized. The streets were calling and he was hustling from sun up to sun down. St. Louis was experiencing the worst winter ever and Asia couldn't handle the neglect. When Brandon had made the phone call, she let him know that it was time to end their relationship. He let her know he would come pick her up and they could talk about it.

Asia let her aunt and uncle know that she was about to leave with Brandon. She felt the need to let them know who she was with every time she left home. They never questioned her and never hounded her. As long as everyone was there to sit down for dinner, the rest of the time was irrelevant.

Brandon had picked up Asia as he said he would, but with a car full of people in his green four door 1989 Cutlass. One of the backseat passengers got out and let Asia get in. Now the Cutlass occupied six passengers instead of the allowable four. Asia noticed two familiar faces. She noticed Brandon's friend Stacks and his girlfriend Robin. Brandon drove north on Grand Avenue making a left onto Lee Avenue and a quick right onto John Avenue and dropped off two of his passengers.

Once out of the car, Brandon proceeded back onto Grand Avenue, taking it south until he reached Natural Bridge Avenue; taking Natural Bridge Avenue to Union Avenue to the Walnut Park area; known to most St. Louisians as Muderville. He pulled in front of Stack's house on Davidson Avenue.

Stacks lived with his father and sister, Melody. Stack's father was an over the road truck driver who left his children to raise themselves.

Once in the house, everyone sat down in the living room. Melody came down with an energetic smile welcoming home her brother and his long time friend, Brandon. Heading toward the kitchen, she offered everyone drinks. Being in the

Midwest with southern hospitality was a bit odd, so Asia and Robin jumped on the opportunity.

The house was immaculate. The kitchen was tidy and items were arranged neatly. There was nothing extravagant, but the cleanliness made things appear to be comfortable.

The girl's chitchatted. Asia wasn't engaged in most of the conversation piece. She only got down with Shante like that. She would giggle every time something funny was said.

Asia headed back to the living room. Once she entered, Robin soon followed. She left Melody talking on the phone in the kitchen.

Robin and Stacks headed upstairs for some quality and alone time. Brandon cut on the television and Asia became irritated. It appeared that he was avoiding the conversation she insisted on having. Asia was not sure if he didn't want to talk or if he knew that, she was breaking it off.

Brandon led Asia upstairs to Stack's father bedroom. The room was overwhelmed by the bulkiness of the king size waterbed. Brandon sat down on the red satin fitted sheet. His body had a slight movement as the water shifted. Asia stood there in the doorway looking at his constant movement.
"Shut the door." Brandon spoke seductively.

"What I need to shut the door for?" Asia rolled her eyes and folded her arms across her chest.

"Shut the door and find out." Brandon laid back and the wave-like motion shifted his body slowly.

"Who room is this?" Asia waited on his answer, still positioned in the doorway. She could hear the moaning sounds, which were taking place two doors down from where she was standing.

"It's ours right now." Brandon wiggled his blue jean pant down around his thighs. His manhood was fighting against his green plaid boxers.

Asia watched him as he pulled his shaft from the small incision of his boxers. With a rolling of an eye and a look down the hall, she shut the door. She lay down beside him and took control of his magic stick as she began to stroke his hard on.

The rhythm of the movement of the water caused them to struggle in the connection of their mouths meeting. Brandon rolled over and tried to lie on Asia's shifting body. After tussling in the removing of each other's clothing, together they laid there nude in each other's embrace. Asia was ready. She knew it wasn't about to be painful because he wasn't working with much. The little he was working with, he knew exactly what to do with it and what his shaft wouldn't do, his tongue worked it out exceptionally. Since he had stepped his head game up form their first oral encounter.

The sex escapades were done and the couples were back down stairs occupying the living room quarters. When Robin fronted Stacks of his quickie and her being gypped, he bopped her in her mouth. She then tried to put up a fight and Stacks quickly brought that to an end when he hit her with all his might. When she fell back into the sofa shielding her from the next blow, it was over before she knew it.

All the commotion brought Melody out the kitchen.

Stacks was now ready to go. Brandon said his goodbyes to Melody and led the crew to his car in silence. They walked in a single file line following each other in the clear pathway. The winds were low and the temperature didn't feel as cold as the snow made it appear to be. He wasn't ready to drop off Asia, but he wasn't ready to be alone with her either.

"Are you hungry?" Brandon looked at Asia as he was about to turn onto Natural Bridge. She let him know that she was and Taco Bell was the best suitable choice.

Once on Taco Bell's parking lot, Brandon handed Asia a twenty-dollar bill. She got out the car asking the occupants of the car if they wanted anything. No one said anything, but Robin got out and followed her into the restaurant.

Brandon was in clear view of the entire restaurant. He noticed Asia and Robin looking to their left once they made it through the doors. He directed his attention to the four guys that sat in the dining area. So he watched as he could tell that a conversation was taking place amongst the guys and his girl.

He grew frustrated as he sat and watched four football playing looking dudes draped in jewelry smiling while engaged in a conversation with Asia. One even pulled out a bankroll and Asia walked over to the table and took some money from the person that appeared to be the leader. He was wearing the most jewelry, the diamond bezel letter C that hung from his gold rope chain indicated his status, and he was the only one that sat in the restaurant without a coat.

Asia exited the restaurant with her Taco Bell bag and a phone number written on a hundred dollar bill. When she made it over to the car, she noticed that Brandon was now sitting in the back seat and Stacks was behind the steering wheel. Asia and Robin both got in the back seat.

"Asia, when was the last time you talk to Andre?" Brandon looked at her as she pulled her food out the bag and took a bite.

Asia didn't know how to answer the question because she wanted to know what brought that about. She figured all the time they had to talk, he didn't grasp the opportunity, and so she wasn't worried about talking now, especially anything that had to do with Andre. Asia had already decided early on that this would be the last day Brandon would hear from her. Thinking about his question, she wanted to tell him that she had talked to Andre everyday this week. He would be home because the semester had ended and he wanted to spend his break with her.

Asia looked at Brandon and swallowed her food, "He will be home on my last day of school before winter break."

"You gone fuck him, too?" Brandon looked over at Asia in a hard stare.

Asia's face wore a frown. For some reason the comment affected an unknown emotion of Asia's. She had just giving herself to him. That moment was special, at least to her for that time. She thought about how she was about to answer his question. She wanted him to feel the cheap feeling she was undergoing in presence of others in the car.
"I just might, his dick is bigger than yours!"
The words flowed from her mouth as if it was as though she sang the bigger than yours words.

Stacks had jumped due to Brandon making a sudden shift and knocking the shit out of Asia. Tacos went flying and Robin was now wearing lettuce, cheese, and ground beef along with her bruised face.

Stacks had pulled in front of Brandon's house. Brandon and Stacks got out and entered the house in front of the parked car. Asia was helping Robin rid herself of the flung food. Once that was done, Asia decided that it was time for her to go. She hopped in the driver's seat; put the car in reverse, and a loud boom filled the air.

The car was parked on a pack of ice. Once she shifted the car in reverse and applied the break, the car slid. Brandon and a slew of other people poured out of nearly every house on the block. When he saw that Asia had back into a fire hydrant, he laughed. Asia was uneasy. She was tensely frozen up. Robin looked at her as if she was in this fight alone. Asia wished that Shante were there.

Preparing for the worst, Asia watched Brandon as he opened the driver side door, "Are you ready to go or something?"

Asia was ready for the attack. Nothing happened. Brandon didn't do a thing. He didn't even ask a question. He just drove her home. When she got out the car, Brandon told her not to forget to call him before she goes to bed. Asia knew she was not calling him, but she felt the need to show him instead of telling him.

It was a task getting rid of Brandon. Her family was growing tired of lying; telling him, she was not there, but they did as she asked. When she was on the phone, she didn't take the time to answer. Brandon's voice was the last voice she wanted to hear. Asia went as far as missing a few days of school and leaving early when she did go. Shante let her know how Brandon was out on the prey. When Shante let her know that, she hadn't seen him in a couple of days, Asia decided to go back to school. Thinking that Brandon had given up on finding her and having the need to get her schoolwork, she decided to go school. It was the last day before Christmas break and she needed to make up the work.

Asia and Shante walked out of the school. Brandon noticed the diamond bezel letter C before he saw Asia's face. Asia was glad that the bus pulled up right as they were walking out of the building.

Asia and Shante ran across the street to get the first seats on the bus. School buses were not provided. You used either public transportation, walked, or had your own means of transportation.

Brandon looked around to see if he saw the owner of the chain. When he noticed that Asia was boarding the bus, he hopped out of his car.

Asia had slowed down and let two other girls go after Shante. It was three boys boarding with them so she placed herself inline in front of the boys. As she handed the bus driver her bus ticket she felt someone's hand in the top of her head grabbing her by her hair. The tight grip was preventing her from turning her head, as her body was being drug off the bus. Reaching the bottom of the steps, she saw the butt of the gun that Brandon had tucked in his waistband. When Shante noticed Asia not behind her, it was too late. She looked around and saw Asia being forced in Brandon's car.

Brandon didn't say a word, although he wanted to. He was curious to why Asia was wearing this chain. Had she had her coat buttoned up, he wouldn't have noticed it.

Asia didn't know how to feel. She knew it was nothing he could say to her that would work things out. No man had ever laid a hand on her. Uncle Rob never spanked, pinched or punched her. The father she never knew wasn't around to do any type of discipline.

Fear start to set in. She sat and watched the rode as Brandon drove around. When darkness fell upon this winter day, he headed home. As he pulled in front of his house, Asia convinced herself she was going to put up a fight so that everyone would know she was outside. The gun persuaded her to go quietly.

For seven days and seven nights, Brandon kept Asia hostage in his basement bungalow. The room had no windows and on the opposite side of the door was a lock. Asia felt as though she was in the pit of hell. He would bring her food and she would not eat. She didn't bathe in the shower that was housed in the room. She figured Brandon wouldn't want to have sex if she was dirty, but he didn't care. He did his thing and went right to sleep. He would lay slumped on Asia and if she moved, he'd wake up.

Everyone was looking for Asia. Robert's method of the doctor worked the same way with the police. He figured she was bound to run off since her mother did. Shante was afraid to tell who she was with. Asia being in some real danger never once crossed her mind. Andre was now looking for her. He wondered why she would perform a disappearing act when she knew he was coming home. He thought she had no real way of finding out what he was doing in Jackson, Mississippi. Although a few people who attended high school with the both of them, attended Jackson State also. None was friends with Asia so he figured word hadn't gotten back home on how he was partying. His conscience was tearing him apart. When he asked Shante, she let him know the truth. She informed him that she hadn't heard from Asia. She didn't want to tell on her girl, but she was going to kill Asia herself for worrying the hell out of her.

Brandon had stepped out to check on his money. He couldn't be out on the set as much; being he had occupied himself with a new hobby of kidnapping. He took Asia's coat, clothes, the chain, and shoes with him when he left the first time to check on his money. He left all the items in his car. Brandon's plan was returning the items and Asia home once he knew Andre was back at Jackson State.

Asia cried a river. She was being physically taunted. Brandon never said as much as two words. He was just having himself such a good time taking full advantage of her. She lay crying the entire time. She was growing angry in her heart. It all stemmed from her being angry with her mom, the dad she never met, and the fact she was at a disadvantage.

When the door began to open, she was thinking of knocking him down and running out. She saw Harold, Brandon's older brother standing in the doorway. Harold looked her over and instantly knew something wasn't right. She wasn't the neatly groomed young lady he had seen with his brother on a few occasions. He remembered her just from her classy appearance. When she asked him to take her home, he obliged. She was dressed in one of Brandon's jogging suits and a pair of his tennis shoes.

The minute she walked in the door looking the way she did, her uncle grew furious. He decided he would wait for her to tell him where she had been. He held her as she cried like a newborn baby. He figured once the Brandon calls stopped, he figured that might have been where she had been. He was unsure if she was hiding from Andre, but when he saw her, he knew she was being held against her own will. Uncle Robert never asked a single question.

######

Asia stood up looked around at all the boxes. She moved some things around to plug in the television. Good thing she hadn't called to get the cable disconnected because her television wouldn't have had a signal.

Once the television was on, she walked over to the closet, reached for the top shelf and removed the St. Louis Cardinals blanket she always kept there. Walking back over to the couch, she picked up her cell phone and stared at the notebook that was now lying on the floor. She called Andre and didn't get an answer.

When he saw the call come through he didn't press ignore, he placed the phone back in its clip and proceeded in the building.

"Good Evening, Detective Townsend," The guard spoke as he entered.

Detective Townsend kept right on walking. If he opened his mouth, he knew his hurt would just pour out. He slightly nodded his head to acknowledge the individual who had acknowledged him.

After being ignored by Andre, Asia then tried Shante.

"Hello." Shante knew exactly who it was because Asia's

ring tone was *Buddy* by De La Soul. All that heard the ring tone would criticize her for having an old song that didn't comply with the relationship of what she and Asia had. It fitted its purpose for Shante because Asia was her buddy.

When Asia didn't say a word, she knew something was wrong. Shante waited. She could hear a few muffles. She was not ready for whatever her friend had to tell her, "Asia, what's wrong."

"Andre saw the list." Asia sat silently.

Shante didn't know what to say. She had told Asia when she made the list, which was something that didn't need to be wrote down or even thought about. It was a thing of the past and that is where it needed to stay. She even told Asia that a lot of things that happen on the radio make people want to voice their opinion, but she refused due to not wanting anyone to recognize their voice, so they just keep it moving. She didn't know what to say because all she could think of was, "I told you so."

"Asia, give him some time to calm down. Shit, did he even know what the list meant?" Shante waited on Asia.

"Shante, it doesn't take a rocket scientist to figure it out. You saw it." Shante thought about when she held the notebook. The list was numbered with several male names.

"You should have told him those were people you were inviting to the wedding." Shante laughed.

Asia wanted to laugh but she couldn't bring herself around to it. She didn't find any humor in it. Andre had become the man she had always dreamed of. All her life, she had prayed for someone like him. He was close to her like the father she'd always prayed for. She thanked the man above for having a man of his caliber in her life. Andre was in her every thought. All the men she had met, he had been the only person whom she had ever loved. His actions showed that he felt the same way about her. The day he came into the precinct and proposed to her, she nearly sexed him in front of all their coworkers.

"I'm on my way over. I'm going to stop and get some of that Red Velvet wine and I'll be there shortly." Shante hung up without waiting on Asia to respond.

Asia was surprised that Shante's choice was as smooth as inexpensive wine. The drink of choice during pain and sorrow was Crown Royal a simple taste that would be acquired from two young girls sneaking a drink whenever Shante's mother turned her back.

Shante had a phone call to make. She pulled in front of the liquor store waiting on Andre to answer his phone. He ignored her, a couple of times but she was persistent. He finally answered.

"Shante, there is nothing you can say to me." Andre was about to hang up although he wanted to call her a long time ago. He was glad she reached out first.

"Dang! Slow your roll. Can I get a hello? You and Asia need to talk. I don't know what took place. All I know is that my girl is in some major pain and I don't like it. Dre, you better than that. You need to hear her out."

"Tae! Hear her out." Andre refers to Shante as Tae from time to time, "Man, everybody in St. Louis done ran up in that. Here I am walking around with a beautiful arm piece that everybody done knocked down. Do you know who I am? People in this city know me."

"Whatever it is you are talking about shouldn't even matter. Y'all about to do the damn thing and you ain't ever met anybody like Asia. That was way before you." Shante had said the wrong thing and she knew it. She was trying to figure who in the city knew and remembered him beside the individuals he may have arrested.

"Tae, I was the first to run up in that and thought I was the only one. I was about to take a hoe down the lane and change her last name. She ain't kept it real with me. Asia's been keeping secrets the whole time." Andre shook his head.

"Andre, don't know body know you. You left the school in '96 yo ass been WASHED UP every since. All that all-American bullshit didn't get you anywhere. Yo ass ain't nothing but a punk ass policeman from the hood. Besides, that was twelve years ago. How many hoes you done hit that my girl don't know about?" Shante hung up her phone. That was not her plan for the conversation. She knew she should have rehearsed something for Asia's defense.

Chapter 7

CALEB

"Speak to Caleb?" Asia waited on Caleb to come to the phone.

"May I ask whose calling?" asked the individual on the other end of the phone line.

"Asia." she said.

"Caleb! Asia is on the phone!" the phone fell and bumped up against something ending with a couple of bangs echoing through the receiver. Footsteps walking toward the phone were the next sound that was heard.

"LO." Caleb uttered.

"This Asia."

"Where you been? I called you a couple of times. Got a nigga chain and shit. That's all you wanted? I could have bought you your own." Caleb waited to hear what she had to say.

"You can come get your chain. I didn't ask you for it anyway. You came to my house, stood outside, and before you pulled off you put your chain around my neck. Besides, if all I wanted was your chain I wouldn't be calling you now!" Asia shook her head. She was not about to deal with any more games.

"My bad. What's up with you?" Caleb questioned.

"I was calling to see what was up with you." Asia wanted to get out the house. She had been in the house since December. As far as she went was across the street to talk with

Shante and to school.

As soon as it had gotten warm, Brandon rode down the street as they sat on the porch. Uncle Robert would ask about him every now and then. He had thoughts of taking care of Brandon. He taunted with himself because Asia never confided in him exactly what had happened. Robert sometimes thought Asia did a lot of things to gain attention because that's usually what his sister did when they were young.

Shante and Asia just looked at Brandon as he rode by with Stacks's sister, Melody, in the car with him. A few minutes later, he came back around and threw Asia's clothes in the street. She was rendered speechless when she saw that he hadn't kept Caleb's chain.

During the entire time Asia called herself hibernating, she had not gained the courage to speak with Andre yet. She was still avoiding him. It was mainly due to the fact that they had shared each other's deepest secrets and this was a secret she knew she was never going to tell him.

When Caleb pulled up, Asia was already standing outside. She didn't want her family seeing Caleb just yet. He occasionally rolled through after the first time Asia asked him to come over and they sat in front of her apartment building talking for hours. He enjoyed the fact that she had dreams. He would even make suggestions for the clothing line she dreamed about establishing.

Asia walked up to his black '95 Audi. She opened the car door. "Where are you trying to take me?" she looked him over, thinking he is too tall for this car. This dude needs a Cadillac, a truck, or something. His ass is too damn big for this car. Caleb was every bit of six foot seven with a thirteen-size shoe. Asia loved the fact he was as chocolate as Andre was.

He smiled at her. He was glad to see Asia wearing his chain. He spent four stacks on the diamond bezel C. With the chain, he was out of seven grand. He wasn't a major player in the game but he was eating.

"I figured we'd go to the movies and see that new Ice Cube movie, Anaconda." Caleb waited on Asia to get in.

It was such a coincidence that Asia had on a solid red Ralph Lauren tee with Khaki Ralph Lauren shorts and red Polo canvas shoes. Caleb had on a stripe red, black and white Polo shirt, tan Khaki's, and some red and black Nikes. Asia got in and he drove off bumping his Notorious B.I.G.'s *Life After Death*.

The movie was fine and the summer was twenty-one days away. Caleb was surviving. He still hadn't met the family, but he felt comfortable enough to take her to his mother's house.

Asia thought this was something special, too special for her. It was time to cut Caleb short. She hadn't taken the time to pay attention to him edge wise. She would have known that he lived with his grandmother. His mother had the spot where he worked from. Every chic he met went this place.

Asia had gotten tired, went, and laid across the bed in the one bedroom apartment Caleb's mother occupied. She was waiting on him to take her home. Moments later, he was there besides her kissing up her thighs. She was undressed and Caleb was barely in.

Asia opened her eyes. All the things she heard about tall guys and big feet was a lie. This was pure disappointment.

He was a lot smaller than Brandon was.

"You wanna ride this dick baby?" Caleb panted like a dog in heat.

"No! The only ride I want is to go home." Asia pushed him up and stood up to put her clothes back on.

Asia shook her head, "Six foot three and hung like a flea!"

Asia suddenly opened her eyes. She lay on the sofa. She began to look around because she thought she heard someone knocking. As she was about to close her eyes, the knocking started back.

"How long have you been knocking?" Asia asked.

Shante walked in. "I haven't been out there long." She walked toward the kitchenette area to grab some glasses for the wine.

Asia went to find Shante a blanket from the boxes. She cracked the box open marked blankets and pulled out a denim Tommy Hilfiger comforter. Asia sat on one end of the white leather sofa while Shante occupied the other end.

Looking at the floor, Shante sipped on her wine. "Why the hell you still got this out for?" Shante slightly bent over to pick up the notebook.

Shante looked over at her friend, "Asia, remember when you said you wanted to be a fashion designer? You need to use this paper to start some sketches and burn these names." Asia looked at Shante she couldn't bring herself to even smile.

She always thought of designing a line of jeans but to her it was only a thought. She couldn't believe that Shante still remembered that she told her that. Now that she was going through what she felt like some turmoil, she figured she could put her energy toward a dream but the desire was not even there.

Chapter 8

YESTERDAY

Shante stood in front of the vanity looking in the white oval shaped bathroom mirror. She noticed a small pimple on her smooth brown skin. She was not about to bust it so it wouldn't leave an ugly blemish on her skin. She put a small dab of toothpaste on the bump. That pimple was the least of her worries. Perching her lips, she blew a kiss to herself. The smile she wore quickly became a frown. The reflections that glanced back at her were a little girl crying inside. Growing up in a household that she wasn't comfortable in was beginning to take a toll on her no matter how far from it she was. The pain was not seen because she appeared to have very thick skin. Her main problem was the responsibility of her sister, Shannon.

Shannon was the worst child she had ever met. She got into all kinds of mess. She went about life as if she didn't have a care in the world. When Shannon was about three or four, she had drunk a small amount of bleach. Shante could smell it on her. Shante panicked. She knew that her mother would be pissed if she found out. She would call her everything under the sun. Shante called the poison center. She informed the operator that she was doing some homework and she wanted to know what to do if a child had drank some bleach. The operator told her to take the child to the emergency room or give the child some milk. She didn't know if the milk was the best thing on top of bleach, but she wasn't about to have

Shannon rushed to the emergency room on her watch.

She gave Shannon a small glass of milk. Shannon vomited all over Shante and the floor. Shante hastily cleaned up the mess. She kept a close eye on Shannon. Shante was not going to let Shannon go to sleep. Shante would doze off and wake up to make sure Shannon was still breathing. The next day came and Shannon seemed fine. Shante was so glad. That petrified feeling she had all day had finally left. She put every item she thought was poison out the reach of Shannon.

Shante was Shannon's protector. The only protection that Shante needed was to keep from getting into any trouble. If Shante's mother told them not to come inside and Shannon went in away, Shante would be in some major trouble. Shante never allowed her to go inside out of fear of what could happen to her. She had an idea to what was taking place when she and her sister were sent outside when her mother's visitors would stop by.

The day Asia walked into her life, Shante finally found what she considered to be her outlet. Asia and Shante immediately formed a bond. One day out of the blue Shante cried profusely. Asia didn't say a word. She just hugged her tightly and let her cry. That one hug communicated affection amongst them both. Asia had listened with her eyes and with her heart. It allowed her to hear Shante completely. This mutual sharing grew them closer together. Many days came when they would just cry together without expressing why. Eventually, they got around to discussing their childhood. Listening to each other's semantics, they knew they couldn't be much different.

Without acknowledging it, the girls had accepted the fact that their home characteristics were inadequate. Over the years, they began to accept their lifestyles as a reality. Shante withdrew from her mother totally. She turned to Asia for help and received protection and empathy. Asia's protection distanced Shante even further from potential friends. Asia was all the friend that she needed.

From the outside looking in, no one would ever be able to tell that Shante or Asia's home life was on the blinks. With each other, nothing else mattered. They would sneak each other into their room and stay up talking about the latest fashions, boys, and having a double wedding when they found their prince charming. When conversations arose about kids, no one wanted any, but if it happened, they promised never to treat their children the way their mothers' had treated them. They decided that after they established themselves in the fashion industry children would come afterwards. It was no need in bringing extra mouths in the world that would be a hassle to feed.

Shante stood looking in the mirror. All she could do was smile. She was so glad that Asia had come into her life. Although her pain didn't disappear, Asia's companionship was a bearer from Shante's mother ridicule and hurt. Meanwhile, Asia found herself holding all her hurt inside. She had adopted a false view of herself. Asia would act as if she was considerably superior to all others. She held back a lot of pain as well. Shante couldn't believe the strength that she saw in Asia, but she was glad that she had it. She had to be strong for her little sister, Shannon. After Shannon would cry on her shoulder, Shante would go running to cry on Asia's shoulder. She appreciated Asia. The moment she found her mate she was going to make, them love her. She planned to sacrifice and do what it took to make them love her. Her love was going to be strong enough to the point they would not get tired of her and leave. Deep down in her heart she wanted to find that special someone that could make her life complete and so content.

Her mother stated very often that a women with a vagina that knows how to use it, was a very wealthy women. She would never forget when her mother violated her. She was about to go outside to meet Asia. When Asia knocked on the door, Shante had to run to the bathroom. When she came out the restroom, her mother stood in a drunken stance and grabbed her crouch as soon as she opened the door. She looked her directly in her eyes. Shante could smell the alcohol on her mother's breath as she held her crouch tightly, "As long as you have this, you are sitting on a money maker. You should never be broke!" Asia wasn't there but she must have had heard that before, Shante thought to herself. Her mother telling her to use what she had to get what she want and talking about her father was something she just couldn't forget.

Her mother could never give her a straightforward answer about the whereabouts of her father. The last time she asked her mother about her father was the last time she would ask her anything about this stranger. Her speech was very slurred. She replied, "Go over there and get the phonebook."

Shante ran and got the phonebook. She was so excited. She knew her mother was going to look him up and give him a call. She didn't know if her mother was going to have her look for the number or just look for it herself. Shante smiled as she was finally about to get the name and the number of her father. Shante was about to hand her mother the phone book. Her mother never looked up. With slurred speech she said, "You look in the phone book and let your fingers do the walking. You pick one that sounds like he could be your daddy and let me know." She really couldn't tell her because she didn't know herself.

Her mother happened to find some humor in her statement. Her drunken slur turned into a burst of laughter. Shante was experiencing heartache and pain. Shante couldn't believe she was laughing. She didn't find anything funny about that. Shante knew that when her mother was full of alcohol she was bound to say anything. There wasn't many times that Shante's mother was sober. It was a very sad situation. Through all the drama, Shante still had love for her mother. The love was what kept her from killing her mother.

Chapter 9

DILLIAN

Shante grinned at the notebook, "Dillian and Darnell. Girl, remember when you said you were going to have Dillian's baby, all because he had some good hair. His ass looked exactly like that old school rapper Special Ed. Especially, with that curly ass hair."

"That dude was special. I ain't never said shit about having his baby. I was not about to bring a baby in this world out of wedlock. My child would never be able to be called a bastard!" Asia shot back with a laugh.

"You know you wanted that man's baby!" Shante almost spilled her wine from laughing.

Asia looked toward the ceiling leaning her head back on the sofa.

######

It was Asia's last year of high school. The last two weeks of summer had arrived and she had finally got in touch with Andre without him asking any questions. They spent some time together before he went back to school.

She expected him to make mention of her absence

when he came home for winter break. It was not a big deal to him. He thought Asia might ask why he didn't come home for Spring Break. Now they both had secrets.

Asia couldn't wait until Andre had left. She was very interested in being introduced to Tara's Cousin.

"Asia, you wait till you meet my cousin, Dillian? He's cute. Y'all about the same complexion. Come to think about it, you two even smile alike." Tara was doing as instructed. Her cousin wanted her to hook him up with somebody that went to her school.

Asia looked Tara over. Asia thought she was a pretty girl. She was bright as day with soft black long luxurious hair. Asia figured good looks must have run in Tara's family.

Tara stayed around the corner from Asia and Shante. The entire four years of high school, they never had conversation for one another. The way Asia and Shante, dressed put them semi-close to her level. Tara was a step above. BCBG, Via Spiga, and Gucci was in her wardrobe. She was messing around with a major player in the dope game by the name of Gavin, who financed it all.

After school, Asia and Shante went over Tara's house. Shante wasn't going to be able to stay long because she had to complete some paperwork for the job in collections she had been hired for last week. Shante tried to get Asia to go with her, but Asia said as long as she didn't work her uncle would keep the funds coming. It wouldn't be long before the clothing assistance allowance program would end. Asia's Aunt Wanda stumbled across the Mers Goodwill. This little program called "Dress for Success" kept Asia looking good.

Shante looked over at Asia. She knew if circumstances were reversed and Asia was asking her, she would have jumped on the opportunity.

Shante was hooked up with the latest fashions because her mother's baby sister that was five years older than Shante was a booster. She could steal your eyeballs when you winked.

If Tara knew in the beginning that Asia was the leader of the two, she would have hooked Shante up. Dillian just wanted some pussy anyway. Tara had been caught with her hand in the cookie jar when Dillian was in one of Gavin's dope houses one day. Tara and Gavin had stopped by before they had gone to the movies. When Gavin went to release his bladder, Tara was taking some of Gavin's ends. This wasn't the first time and Dillian let that be known that he had seen her before.

The girls sat on Tara's front porch. When the gray '77 LTD Landau pulled up, Asia was lost for words. She was not ready for any bum ass boys. Dillian stepped out the car with Gavin. Asia looked them over once and could smell the money. Asia made it her business to stay up on the latest trends. It was very much needed if she and Shante ever wanted to get into the fashion industry. Asia stayed abreast on the fashions from reading Vogue and Esquire magazines. Shante just let Asia educate her on the fashions.

Gavin was wearing black denim Ecko Untld jeans with the new Black Bally Stad man sneakers and a white Stafford tee. Asia could tell by the thickness of the T-shirt that it was Stafford. Gavin and Dillian could pass for brothers, although Gavin was darker than Dillian. Gavin looked to appear to have some Haitian in his bloodline. Gavin's eyes were hazel. This was a first for Asia. She had never seen someone this complexion with hazel eyes. His slender frame was an added attraction. Asia, somehow, winded up attracting the chubby dudes lately and they were coming up short. Asia's eyes were on Tara's man. The way he walked was just part of his swag.

Asia turned her attention directly to Dillian. He was wearing white Bally Stad man sneakers with burgundy stripes and denim jeans with faded spots on the thigh area. She couldn't make out the brand, but she was about to check it out. He had the athletic build going on like Andre.

"I know you." Dillian pointed to Asia while taking a seat on the concrete sitting area near the door on the porch.

Gavin walked up and kissed Tara on the cheek.

"Where you know me from?" Asia looked back at Dillian with her heart shape lips poking out.

"You um that dude's girl that played basketball, baseball, football, and ran track, for Beaumont." Dillian nodded his head.

"How you know me though?" Asia wanted to know. She knew she attended most of Andre's games, missing a few here and there.

"Girl everybody from my basketball team would talk about you and yo partner right here." Dillian pointed to Shante, "You and yo partner walked through the gym with such confidence demanding everyone's attention. Y'all got that, "my shit don't stink" type of walk. That shit's top notch!" Dillian nodded his head with a smile.

Tara rolled her eyes. Asia and Shante shared a laugh. They both were impressed that Dillian had notice them at a few games. That was their sole purpose for walking around all the time, just to be seen.

"I'm ma get up with you all a little later." Shante stood up to leave, "Y'all could have brought a friend for me."

"Don't leave! We can call somebody for you." Dillian looked at Shante very seductively.

"My bus comes in the next ten minutes and I have something important to take care of." Shante began walking off the porch.

"Dee, can take you!" Gavin yelled.

"Yeah, I can take you." Dillian thought Shante was the person he was there to see. Asia thought Greg was bringing somebody for her, so this threw her for a loop. "Asia, you going to go with them?" Tara asked.

It didn't take long before Dillian realized that Asia was the one his cousin had chosen for him.

Asia was fine with Shante and Dillian hooking up. Tara was the one that needed to be concerned. Asia had her eye on Gavin for the most part.

"We can swing by and pick up Darnell. He out on the block." Dillian started walking toward the car, "Where do you have to go?"

"I'm going out to Earth City." Shante followed Asia and Dillian to the car.

"You got time for me to go over on Thomas to pick up, Darnell?" Dillian asked.

"I got plenty of time. It would have taken me an hour and half to get to Earth City by bus." Shante said as she got in the car.

"A, Dee!" Dillian yelled toward Darnell.

He was standing near a lamppost in the middle of Thomas with a group of hard looking dudes that look like they were up to no good.

Darnell strolled over to the car. Shante looked him over and was pleased. He had on his thick clean crisp Stafford white tee, black Jordan basketball pant, and some black Jordan tennis shoes. She could see his bulge and could tell he was hung. When he opened his mouth, he had a mouth full of gold teeth. His hair was pulled back in a ponytail.

"Come ride with me." Dillian said all smooth.

Darnell got in the backseat with Shante.

"Which one of you knows how to braid?" Darnell rubbed his hands through his hair.

Asia looked back at him. She had to get a good look at him in the car. The way he strolled over to the car, he looked like Alonzo Harris. The character Denzel Washington played in the movie, "Training Day." Except that, he had hair instead of the low cut.

"Shante knows how to braid." Asia answered his question.

The car ride was full of conversation. The radio was there but when Asia turned the knob, nothing happened. Dillian told her it didn't work and the radio was there just for a front. With a few twist and turns of the knob, he pulled the area out where the radio, ashtray, and space for heating and cooling were hollow. It was occupied with a thirty-eight snub nose and couple of packages containing a hard solid white substance. Asia thought to herself, "How stupid?! Why in the world did he want me to see that?"

Shante came back out. She had a few papers in her hand. She got in the car and she let Asia know she would only be working on weekends. After graduation, she had the opportunity to work full-time.

On the way back to the city, Dillian made a pit stop at Northwest Plaza. He parked near the door where Famous and Barr Department Store was located. Going through the main entrance of the mall, Dillian led them to Harold Penner's House of Fashion. Harold Penner's had the newest fashions from New York.

Asia watched as Dillian pulled out his wad of cash. She was impressed with his bankroll. When he told her to pick something out for herself, she didn't hesitate. Parasuco jeans and matching tee was her choice. She even picked up Shante a pair of Enyce jeans and matching tee. When she told Shante to come with her to try it on, Shante knew what was up.

A whole month went by and Dillian was wining and dining Asia. Shante had hooked up with Darnell a couple of times. He made sure to call her every time he needed his hair braided. With Shante's work hours, Asia didn't get to see her as much on the weekends.

Dillian picked Asia up from her house. He had to make a few runs before they were headed to their destination. He pulled up at the gas station and got out the car to pay for the gas. While he was paying for the gas, a gray four door BMW pulled up. Dillian walked out but turned back around, going back into the station. The driver of the BMW walked up to Asia's side of the car as he was headed toward the inside of the store. He threw a piece of paper in the window. She caught it as though nothing happened.

He walked in front of the car. Asia held the piece of paper up to let him know she had it. Asia nodded looking at his number and watching his loose cream linen shorts move pass the LTD.

He put up the "call me" gesture near his ear. Asia hadn't seen Ethan since her freshman year. Asia would do his homework every since they were in the sixth grade. Ethan was her first crush.

She heard he was doing big things. His boy, Lotto had St. Louis on lock. His real name was Johnnie but when he started stacking paper, the boys in the hood gave him the name Lotto.

Dillian pulled up on the parking lot of the Airport Marriot Hotel. Asia got out the car after he came out from purchasing the room. Instead of going through the main entrance, they went through the side door.

Dillian cut the television on and got comfortable on the bed. Asia pulled back the comforter and the sheets on the other bed in the room. Sitting on the edge of the bed, she began twirling her feet. Admiring the prettiness of her pedicure, he had gotten earlier she thought about Andre. She knew he would be home and all this fun with Dillian would be cut short. Dillian had just bought her prom dress and accessories. With him around, she didn't need the clothing allowance. He had supplied a completely new wardrobe.

"Raise your ass up and put a hunch in your back. Andre ain't taught you how to fuck!" Dillian was getting irritated as he was trying to do it to Asia doggie style. "I make you look good and I got to teach you how to fuck. You should be throwing this shit to a nigga!" Dillian was killing her insides. She was trying to take it but she didn't want him to know she couldn't handle it, so she was trying to run. Asia was thinking she wouldn't be having sex with him anymore. This was a bit too much for Andre to be trying to follow.

######

"Having his baby was now out of the question. He was way too much for me." Asia thought to herself. She wanted to laugh from the expression Shante was giving her.

"Asia, girl you sleep?" Shante kicked her. "When I go to work tomorrow, I'm going to find Willie's ass. I can't believe he has not called me yet. He does not know, with this Accurient program we have at work, we can find out every address he has ever used. As soon as I get there I'm on that."

Asia just looked at Shante. She didn't have the strength to say a word. Asia was thinking to tell her why bother with looking him up. She knew his club-going ass would be at the Royal Palace. Asia was feeling like all that wrong doing from the past was biting her in the ass right now.

Shante wished she could at least find the words to console her. Asia could see and feel Shante's pain, but she had her own issues. Shante had to do something to help her friend. Shante knew if she were going through something like that, Asia would handle it for her. When Tyrone and Keith had raped her, Asia told Shante that they wouldn't rape anybody else and she took care of that.

Asia's eyes were bloodshot red. All Shante could do was hold her friend to console her. Asia laid her head on Shante's shoulder and Shante kissed Asia on the forehead.

"Asia, it's going to be okay." Shante was going to take care of it. Shante reached for her phone. She didn't wait on him to say hello. When she knew he had answered, she said, "We need to talk. Meet me. I'll call you back tomorrow with the time and place."

Asia wanted to know who that was but she didn't have the energy to ask. For a second she thought it was Willie, but she would have heard his raspy voice through the phone. She knew that the conversation would have went differently.

Chapter 10

ETHAN

Shante held a piece of paper in her hand. She watched as the black F-150 pulled in the parking space right outside of the Culpepper Restaurant. She glanced at the list and the addresses she had gotten from work.

"How are you Detective?" Shante checked him over in his Armani tailored made suit. He removed the jacket and sat down. Of all his family members, he cared about how precise he looked.

The waitress walked over to the table.

"Two Crown Royals with Pepsi." Shante winked at the waitress.

"You still remember." he said.

"Yes, how could I forget? Your choice is the same as my mother's, but that's not what we are here for. Your peeps walked out on Asia. She is not taking it well at all. We need to figure something out to get them back to talking." Shante looked at him with a smirk on her face.

"How's Willie?" the meticulous dressed detective asked.

"How's Crystal?" Shante retorted. Shante knew that Crystal was into the same sex now and he hated that he didn't have full custody of his son.

He nodded his head, "I see where you going with this.

Let's talk about what you called me here for."

Asia walked in the bedroom to run her some bathwater. She knew Shante would be back soon. She wanted to make sure she didn't have any odd smells of funk coming from her body. She had lie on the bare leather sofa and sweated long enough.

She was getting her mouth ready for those good Culpepper's hot wings. Once out the shower she was looking for something to put on. She cracked opened the box marked loungewear. She found her red boy shorts with Tommy sewed across the butt and white Tommy tee. She remembered when Ethan bought it for her.

######

"I haven't seen you since my first year of high school." Asia looked at Ethan as he waited to get his hair cut at *Taylor Made* barbershop. She called him when he was on his way to the barber so she told him she could ride with him. "You know I got put out." Ethan looked at her as if she should know what he was talking about.

"You did. I didn't know that." Asia's facial expression represented a sincere and serious look.

"My dumb ass up in that bitch talking about I was representing Piru Bloods. Those Crips beat my ass in that lunchroom. I went back in that bitch flamin'. I had on my red chucks, red flannel, and had my red flag in my back pocket." Ethan bit down on his bottom lip, "that bitch ass nigga, Brandon, from across the park, came in there and told them something. Little did he know my boys were posted up outside. I had cats out there deep and I'm talking about cats that didn't give a fuck. They were ready to come up in that bitch and murk everything in their way!"

Asia looked at him patiently, waiting on what he had to say next. She had remembered Andre's cousin, Darrell, talking about this. Of all Andre's family members, Darrell dipped in a little bit of everything. When he mentioned Brandon, her antennae went up.

"They left me alone, but Mr. Brown, the principal, called me to the office and let me know that I couldn't come back. He didn't give me suspension or expulsion papers. Mr. Brown just told me that I needed to go somewhere I would fit in. He let me know if I came back I wouldn't be able to go to another public school in the city of St. Louis."

Asia looked at him, "That was probably a good thing."

"It was. I was mad at first. Everybody that was claiming something was claiming Crip up there. It wasn't the safest place for me." Ethan strolled over to the barber's chair.

Asia looked him over. Above all the engines of the hair clippers going and all the barbershop talk that was taking place, she was thinking in her head she could hang out with him. Asia loved the dark coffee complexion of the males' species. Ethan was the coffee in her milk. She just couldn't get with all the hair. He had thick eyebrows. She laughed while looking at his legs. She wanted to tell him to cover them up or at least shave.

Asia looked at Ethan once he was done. His low cut was trimmed up nicely. He had that Steve Harvey hairline going on. Ethan needed to sit longer so the barber could have shaved his entire body. Once he was done at the barbershop, they headed to Northwest Plaza. Asia was hoping that they didn't park near Famous and Barr Department Store. She didn't want to bump into Dillian. Going to the main entrance headed toward the food court, Ethan walked straight to the back. He had talked about this place that had the best pizza. When Asia looked at the Sabarro's sign she thought to herself,

"I know this nigga don't think this place got the best pizza."

Together they stood in line. Ethan asked her did she know what she had wanted. She told him to pick it and she went to grabbed her a seat. She looked out into the crowd. A commotion was going on near Burger King. She could hear someone yelling, "I'm the king and I'm about to have it my way."

The individual was with an entourage. Asia was tuned in. So many cats were trying to become rappers or had become rappers; she wanted to know if a rapper was in her presence. She saw the individual that was the loudest. He walked as though his head was too big for his body. His chin was lying on his chest. All you could see was his teeth when he smiled. The platinum jewelry also lightened up the scene.

Ethan sat the tray, with the pizza on it, on the table, "I didn't know what you wanted to drink, so I got you an orange soda."

"That's fine." Asia took her food off the tray as Ethan handed her some napkins.

They talked over pepperoni pizza and orange soda. When they were finished, Ethan took everything to the trash. Ethan wanted to see if some new tennis shoes were in. So they went in Athlete's Foot.

Leaving Athlete's Foot, they walked over to Dillard's Department Store. Ethan sprayed some Calvin Klein *Escape* on Asia. She liked the smell and he liked the way it smelled on her. Asia walked off as he made his purchase. When he found her, she was looking at the clothes in the junior's department.

He walked right up and start helping her look. When he asked her did she want something else and she said no, he let her know he was going to get her something anyway.

He picked up the shortest shorts he could find. They were bright red with Tommy written across the back. He was trying to find a red shirt to match but they just had white tee shirts.

For almost two weeks, Asia had hung out with Ethan. He had never taken her to his house. Asia was thinking he was homeless or something. They always sat outside one particular house; he only went in to use the bathroom but never invited her in. This had to be the spot because everybody that was outside on the block went in this house. An older woman would come to the door to lookout. Sometimes two little girls that looked about three would stand in the door.

On one particular day Shante and Asia was sitting on Asia's porch when Ethan pulled up. Asia let Shante know it was okay for her to go with them.   They weren't getting ready to do anything but go sit on another porch.

"You watch this nigga sell his dope?" Shante looked at Asia as Ethan walked up to several cars.

"I sit here with him, he make a few sales, and give me a couple dollars. I don't see anything wrong with it. He ain't asking for no pussy or nothing. I'm hanging out, keeping him company. He feed me, clothe me, and put money in my pocket. I can sit here and watch him." Asia looked at Shante.

"I guess." Shante rolled her eyes. She wondered if Asia paid attention to anything she said about her mother. When Shante and her sister were younger, many men came through to see her mother. Her mother never worked a day in her life but she always had money. As a child, she didn't know what was going on, but when she got older, she knew exactly what her mother was doing.

They sat and talked about what they were wearing to prom. Asia told Shante she had all her stuff together. Shante said she was working on it. She had two months remaining. Asia let Shante know she would help her get her prom stuff, if not she would make it herself.

As they sat there and talked, they noticed the street was getting thick. Ethan was barely sitting down. Every time he would go over and sit down on the porch, he would have to get right back up, so he just remained standing on the sidewalk.

"Five-O just rolled pass." Someone yelled from the end of the street.

Ethan went over and had a seat on the porch with Asia and Shante. When the police continued making their presence known, Ethan decided to go in the house.

This was a first for Asia. She didn't know what to expect when she went in. Shante followed behind. Ethan led them to the kitchen area down a long hallway. Every door off the hallway was shut. You could hear televisions playing in a few rooms.

The table was dirty and the four different chairs around the table didn't match anything. The area was clean. It didn't look like much cooking was being done.

Ethan came out one of the rooms rolling a stand with a television and VCR player. He plugged it up next to the refrigerator that was making a low roaring sound.

A few minutes into watching a bootleg copy of The Player's Club with words scrolling across the screen to call this one eight hundred number two little girls ran into the kitchen.

"Y'all hungry?" Ethan asked.

They looked at Asia and Shante and giggled. Asia and Shante just looked. To Asia and Shante, the little girls looked like the kids in the feed the hungry commercials. Ethan got up to follow them when they ran off.

"Are those his little sisters?" Shante waited on Asia to answer.

"I don't think so. He said he don't talk to his mother for some reason. I think those his little cousins. Personally, I think he staying here because he doesn't have anywhere else to go." Asia continued watching the movie.

Ethan walked back into the kitchen, "Y'all want something to eat? I'm getting ready to send my boy to get something to eat."

Asia asked, "Where is he going?"

"I think he is going to McDonald's." Ethan listened to Asia and Shante tell him what they wanted.

The food had arrived and his apple pie was missing. Ethan sent his friend back to get his apple pie. Two hours had passed and the apple pie hadn't arrived. Ethan had put in a new movie and the phone began to ring. His friend called and let him know he had been arrested. Ethan asked Asia and Shante did they want to ride with him to go bail him out.

Shante and Asia gave each other this look. Before Asia could speak Shante spoke up, "We will wait here and watch this movie."

Ethan exited the kitchen. Asia looked at Shante and smiled. Andre's uncle works at the very police station where Ethan's friend is being detained. Asia's presence in Andre's family was well accepted. Shante even felt a part of the family when she went around. They got a kick out of Andre's uncle. He had purple Crown Royal bags for everything.

When Ethan came back, he was talking about how they take too long to do everything downtown. Ethan told Asia and Shante that his friend was taken to the police station due to him not putting his blinker on when he turned back onto the block. He walked over to the television letting the girls know that they were going to his room.

They followed him into one of the closed doors. Entering the room there was nothing but four mattresses stacked on the floor in the middle of the room. Near the window were at least ten black clothes bags. In front of the closet, which had a security door lock and a combination lock securing it was a black chair.

Shante walked over to the chair and sat down. Asia sat down on the mattresses. Ethan lay across the mattress near Asia. Near the top of the mattresses was a six disc stereo. Ethan turned on the stereo, turning the volume down very low. He noticed that Shante had fallen off to sleep while sitting in the chair. Asia had fallen asleep as well. Ethan took his time as he eased his hand up her shirt caressing her breast. Moments later Asia could feel the wetness of his lips around her left nipple.

He took his time unbuckling her belt. Watching to see if Shante was sleeping, Asia assisted in removing her clothes. She noticed he was about to enter and he hadn't put on a condom.

"No balloon, no party." Asia looked at him in the darkness. He hurried out the room. Asia watched Shante as she sat in the chair. She laughed because Shante would sleep in a chair just so she wouldn't mess up her hair.

Ethan came back in ready to party. The party was over before it started.

Shante screamed, "Something just ran across my foot!" she got out the chair, walked over to Asia and lay right next to her. Ethan laid there restless telling Shante that that might have been a mouse. Asia was really ready to go now. Quick sex and rodents was not working for Asia.

Asia opened her eyes and couldn't wait on morning to come. The sun was shining bright through the window that wore a white sheet. She only stayed out because it was a Friday night. She didn't make staying out a habit because she didn't want her uncle worrying.

Asia and Shante walked outside. They walked up the street toward Ethan's car waiting on him to come out. He had a run to make before he dropped them off. Asia was standing there holding the money that he was about to go spend. He had to go back in the house because he had forgotten his scale.

Asia and Shante watched as several unmarked cars pulled up. Numerous bulletproof vest-wearing men dispensed from the cars. They went in Ethan's residence. The first to exit was a man carrying the two little girls. Moments later twelve young boys and the woman that sometime stood in the door exited the house.

Asia couldn't believe that all the people that usually were outside with Ethan were all in the house. In all the conversations, Ethan never told Asia that the place he called home was the crack house.

Ethan's friend that he had sent to McDonald's had told him he was pulled over because of a blinker. He was pulled over because he sold somebody some dope at McDonald's and the police had followed him back to the house. In order to get the heat off him, he gave up everybody by informing the police that the woman who resides at the house allows them to sell dope out of her house.

Asia and Shante walked to the bus stop. They made plans of going to the mall to pick up Shante's prom attire. When she made it home, she called around to find out Ethan's fate.

He buzzed in while she was on hold. He let her know he had violated his parole and he was on the run. He had been wanted for questioning in the murder of Brandon West. Asia was shocked she didn't even know that Brandon had been killed.

Ethan told Asia to tell his sister he had been arrested. He also told her to give his sister half of that sixteen thousand that she was holding for him. He gave her his sister's information and said his goodbyes. Before Asia and Shante headed to the mall, she paid his sister a visit.

Chapter 11

FABIAN

Andre walked in the front door of his ranch style home. He realized that had his parents not had such an influence on him, Asia would have been there with him the entire time. When he came home from college and Asia no longer lived in her uncle's apartment, he wanted to move in with her. His parents didn't believe in shacking. He stayed with his parents until he was able to buy his own home.

Andre undressed removing everything but his boxers. He lay back in his bed. Lost in thought, he wondered if he could move on without Asia. She had been there for him when nobody else was. She was the only one he was not afraid to open up to. He appeared to be the strongest one of the Townsend family. What he couldn't carry, Asia was there to help with the load.

He remembered the day he came home from Jackson during the summer when he had only one year remaining and his parents informed him that his mother had breast cancer. He was distraught when his father told him he was going to have to finish up at an area college because they would no longer be able to finance his last year of school.

The first person he went to see was Asia. The moment

she saw his face she knew something was wrong. He was able to leave his parents with them thinking that he was fine with the suggestion they had just made.

"Asia, I don't want to be like my father and my uncle. Do you know how hard it is growing up with the boys in the hood having cop as a father? Don't nobody trust you. The reason me Darrell, Darryl, Donald and Aaron are so close is because nobody wanted to fuck with us. Darrell tried to dip and dab sometimes and the first time he got caught nothing happened. He was let go because his daddy was a cop. Everybody said he was snitching. Mothafuckas wasn't smart enough to even realize he got off because who his daddy was."

Asia listened to all he had to say. She yearned to have the father that he had. She understood what he was saying. He excelled because he was so concerned with what everybody thought about him. Asia let him know that she would be there for him. Once he told her, he wanted to finish school in Jackson and move away from St. Louis, she let him know she was willing to do everything to help him.

When it was time for him to go back to school, she gave him the money to get back to Mississippi. He let her know that he wouldn't be home for Thanksgiving and Christmas because he didn't want to ask his parents to spend any unnecessary monies. Asia let him know that he didn't have to worry about any money and she would do what she could.

That last year of college for Andre was a breeze. Asia came through for him. She had even sent him a little change to put in his pocket. He didn't even ask where she was getting the money.

Andre picked up the phone to give her a call. Asia laid sleep on the sofa. The Culpepper's hot wings hit the spot. When she heard Keysha Cole's *Sent from Heaven* flaring from her cell phone she jumped up. She flipped it open.

"Hello." Asia said softly. She knew it was him but he hadn't said a word. She knew he wasn't going to say anything. He never would when something was wrong and he was going through something. She would ask what the matter was and he would pour his heart out to her. It was no need to ask what was wrong because she already knew the problem.

Asia began to whisper, "I love you, Andre."

After hearing her voice, he just hung up the phone. He wanted to talk but he didn't know what to say. He thought that had he seen the list alone,   he probably would not have even said anything to her about it. He began thinking about what was his brother and cousins were thinking of him. Asia laid their looking at the next person's name on the piece of paper that had created her dilemma.

######

Two months before school was ending, the loudest person had enrolled in school. As much as he talked and the volume he used when he spoke he couldn't go unnoticed. People said he had gone there before and he had been in the alternative program since his freshman year. He was placed on the list to return to regular school.

Asia heard him as she was about to go to class. He came in right behind her. When he looked at her, he got quiet. Asia remembered seeing him but she couldn't remember where.

When he stood up walking toward the teacher's desk, looking like his head was too heavy to carry, she had remembered seeing him at the mall with his entourage making just as much noise as he was making in the school hallway. He was wearing peanut butter Timberlands and some heavy starched jeans. Asia zoomed right in on his Movado watch.

"Asia somebody is at the door for you!" Uncle Rob yelled.

Shante sat on the edge of Asia's canopy twin bed, without the canopy, while looking through an Esquire magazine as Asia sat in front of her vanity set trying to bump some curls in her hair. They both were trying to figure out who was at the door for Asia. No one had ever popped up without calling.

Shante followed Asia to the door. When Asia walked to the door, she was stunned to see the loud mouth boy at her door.

"How you know where I stay?" Asia held the door and Shante stood behind her with her hand on her hip waiting on him to answer.

"I followed you home. I had been driving up and down this street waiting on you to come out. You were taking so long, I had to knock."

Asia looked back at Shante with a frown of confusing. Turning back to him, "What the fuck do you want?"

"I just want to talk to you." he said.

Shante looked at him, "Why couldn't you wait to talk to her at school tomorrow?"

"I couldn't wait that long." he shot back.

Asia walked outside and Shante followed closing the door. Asia went and sat down on the steps and they all followed.

"So mister, what you want from me?" Asia looked at him.

"You are so pretty. I just want to get to know you." he smiled.

Shante laughed as she watched Asia as she blushed.

"You followed me home?" Asia asked.

"I saw you get on the bus and I followed the bus. When you and her got off the bus, I waited. When y'all had walked for enough, I started walking slowly behind y'all." He said with a serious look on his face.

Asia sat there looking at him with disbelief. She was trying to figure out if he was crazy or not.

"Are you some kind of fool?" Shante barked.

"Naw. I just like nice things." He looked at Asia.

"Well tell me your name." Asia said.

"Fabian." he stated.

Asia and Shante chuckled.

"Y'all wanna go get something to eat?" Fabian questioned.

He didn't know he had said the right thing. These two friends sure could eat. When it came to food, they definitely were not about to turn it down. Asia and Shante followed Fabian over to his brown SS Monte Carlo. Asia held the seat up as Shante climbed in the back.

Fabian pulled up to the Apple Bee's door. He let them out in front and he went and parked the car.

Shante looked from the entrance of the restaurant as Fabian walked toward them, "He looks like a black ass turtle." The girls shared a laugh.

Asia turned to look at him, "He do look like a turtle, girl." Asia tried to stop laughing before he came in the door.

"What are you doing when you get off work?" Asia asked Shante.

Shante held up the phone with her shoulder as she pulled on her pants, "Nothing. Aaron wants me to go with him and Crystal to help her tom boy ass pick out a prom dress."

"What made him call you?" Asia inquired.

"He said he was calling you and you ain't never at home." Shante answered.

"Well that is true. I ain't never here. I'm waiting on Fabian right now. He just picked me up from the beauty shop." Asia looked at herself in the mirror.

"You got that turtle looking motha fucka spending all his doe." Shante laughed, thinking about how Asia had given her five hundred dollars telling her to go buy her something nice, on Fabian.

"You know that boy got a baby." Asia knew Shante didn't know because she had just found out.

"Do he? You mean to tell me somebody let him go up in it raw. Shit he'd a been strapped up just so there wouldn't be a population of black ugly ass turtle's running around." Shante switched the phone to her other ear.

"Girl, he took me over his baby momma's house. He had to drop off some milk. This bitch came running out the house talking about him disrespecting her. I didn't know what the fuck was going on. I just saw him getting out the car with the milk. I was trying to figure out why he didn't drop that off before he picked me up."

"What his baby momma do?" Shante asked.

"She just ran down to the car with the baby in her arms yelling at him. She looked at me and rolled her eyes. She wanted to say something to me but she didn't and I'm glad. That bitch was big as a mother fucka." Asia laughed, "He apologized though. He didn't expect her to come out the door."

"I'll talk to you later. I got to get out of here before I'm late for work." Shante hung up.

"Where you taking me today?" Asia looked over at Fabian.

"I figure we go get us a room and chill." Fabian looked straight ahead. He was using his peripheral vision to see if there was any objection.

Fabian talked about how he was saving his money so that he could get him an apartment. He believed his mother was dipping in and out of his stash. Every time he found a new spot to hide his money, she would find it. She wasn't taking much, but every time he counted it, he was coming up short. He told Asia his baby momma was keeping his money at first, but she would go shopping with it. He didn't have anybody to keep his money for him.

Asia told him it was hard trying to save money. She could put her money up and nobody in her house would touch it. She just had to keep it from herself. It was the truth. Uncle Rob or Aunt Wanda didn't bother her stuff. Keith and Tyrone didn't have enough sense to bother it. She kept all the money she had in the back of the closet in a shoebox.

After listening to Fabian talk, she was curious as to how much money he had. Within the first three months, he had spent ten grand on her. She was going to the beauty shop twice a week and tearing down the malls three times a week. She was about to have to use another shoebox to put her money in.

Asia got up from the bed and went to the bathroom. When she came out the bathroom Fabian was naked. She looked at him thinking that this was not in the plan. She was not about to let him go up in her. Andre would be home in the next couple of days. She didn't feel the need to tell Fabian about Andre. Since he didn't tell her about his child, she planned on letting him find out about Andre the way she found out about his baby.

Fabian turned to the nightstand to turn on the lamp. He rolled back over with a condom in his hand. He grabbed himself to place on the plastic and Asia became moist just by looking at his thickness.

She undressed without him saying a word. Climbing in the bed then onto him, she entered the rodeo at a slow pace. His placed his hand around her waist to guide her to his rhythm.

It was Thursday night. Asia was getting ready for the weekend. After school, she was leaving with Fabian for the weekend. They weren't doing anything special, he just wanted to spend the weekend with her because he had enjoyed himself last weekend. He called and told her to be outside in five minutes, he needed to talk.

Asia walked outside and sat on the porch. She wanted to know why Fabian was speaking with such urgency. Every car that rolled by got her attention. When he turned the corner, she started walking toward the street. She let him park and she got in the car.

He didn't have the worried look that Andre had when something was on his mind. Fabian was wearing a look of fear. His blue tee shirt was all ripped up. From the scratches on his neck, you could tell somebody had grabbed him. He told Asia how his child's mother wouldn't let him leave when he went to see his son. He didn't put his hands on her. She did most of the talking. What Asia got from the conversation is that if she didn't have eight brothers, he would have beaten the shit out of her.

He handed Asia a book bag and told her to hold it for him. He'd be back to pick it up tomorrow. Asia got out the car with the bag placing it on her back and went in the house.

When she got in the house, she had to check the contents in the bag. The money was cool but she didn't know about having drugs in her house. She hid the dope in the back of the closet and began to count the money.

Fabian had left her with fifty thousand dollars. Now, she knew he had some money, but this was out of her league. She was use to petty hustlers with a few thousand dollars. Asia began wondering if that's why he and this girl had gotten in to it.

Friday morning had come. Asia and Shante didn't get the ride from Fabian that they had been getting lately. When they entered the school, something about the atmosphere was strange.

It was gloomy throughout the building. Before first period was over Asia found out why the environment was the way, it was. Fabian had touched so many people in that short time with his comical smile and his loud presence humbled everyone from the students to the staff. Asia was informed that Fabian had been murdered by one of his child's uncles.

Asia had been down and out. When Andre finally came home, she was happy to see him. Then he came to her with his problems. His mother had cancer and his father told him he was going to have to come back home. She reassured him he would be all right. She had saved up some money and she didn't have a problem with helping him out. She didn't understand why he kept bringing it up.

Asia's senior prom had come and gone. The summer was about to end and Andre was on his way back to Jackson. Asia had convinced Andre in letting her and Shante take him back to school. Andre was fine with the suggestion, but there was one problem. Andre was the only one who knew how to drive. Therefore, he was going to tell his brother and one of his cousins to come along. He didn't want them to drive back alone.

When he mentioned it to Aaron, Darrell and Darryl, they all insisted on coming along. Andre rented a seven-passenger van sponsored by Asia.

Asia drove on the highway for two hours. Shante even had the chance to drive. They all got to Jackson, Mississippi in one piece. This was the first time that Shante and Asia had been outside the city limits of St. Louis. They were ready to go back home. Andre wasn't out the van good before they were back on the highway headed home.

Chapter 12

GAVIN

Shante moved about the apartment dodging boxes. She was trying to remain quiet and not wake up Asia. The farthest she had moved from the sofa was to the bathroom. She was glad she had bathed. Had it not been for the braids, her hair would have been all over her head.

Shante was so worried about Asia that she had put her own feelings on the back burner. She thought about going pass Willie's house to see if he was there but she decided against it.

"Asia, I'm leaving for work. Once I get off, I am going to stop by my mother's house. Then I'll come here. Think of what you want to eat today."

Asia opened her eyes, "Okay."

Seconds later, Asia heard a knock on the door. She got up to answer the door wondering why Shante was knocking and she had a key.

"Did you forget something?" Asia opened the door and looked into the image of the Morris Chestnut that she knew, "Aaron why are you here?"

He walked through the door taking a seat on the sofa, "I had to come check on my baby sister. I heard you had lost your mind so I came to help you find it."

"Are you being funny because I don't have time for your jokes," Asia threw the pillow she was holding at his chest. She knew that Aaron envied Andre. He never approached her in a way she or Andre wouldn't approve of. If he had approached her, this would be the one time she would say no. She knew how much love was there. It was just that the spotlight always shined on Andre and Aaron didn't like being in the shadows. His main problem was he didn't know how to get out the shadows. They both resembled each other but Andre's smooth swagger seemed to outshine Aaron's every time.

"I just stopped by to check on you. I went by Dre's house and he didn't answer. I knew he was there because his car was in the driveway. He moping and you definitely moping, y'all just need to talk." Aaron was now regretting he even showed Andre the notebook. He didn't know it was going to go this far. He thought they would share a laugh and it would be over.

Asia couldn't say anything. She didn't know what to say. She didn't know how much Aaron knew about her. She thought she was able to stay low-key the whole time she was doing her thing.

"Asia, I'm getting out of here. I just stopped by. I really hope you and Dre can work this out. You need anything?" Aaron's conscience was bothering him. He felt that had he not pointed the list out, Asia and Andre wouldn't be going through this dilemma. He knew his brother loved Asia dearly. He had to hear how special she was every time Andre went to bed. Aaron kissed Asia on the forehead and walked out the door.

Asia thought about when Aaron was sick and their mother was in the hospital. No one had come to his rescue but her.

"Asia could you please bring me some medicine. I cannot breathe and I'm burning up." Aaron's whining reached out to Asia. She knew his mother was in the hospital and Mr. Townsend most likely was sitting by her bedside.

When Asia got back from dropping Andre off at school, she felt comfortable enough driving that she went out and bought her a car. She was able to pay cash for a '95 two door Chevy Cavalier. After spending five grand, she still had enough tucked away.

Asia pulled into the Walgreen's parking lot. She pulled right next to the four door gray '77 LTD Landau. She went inside the store and got Aaron some Vicks Vapor Rub, Theraflu, Nyquil, and Tylenol. When she got back to her car, the driver of the LTD blew his horn.

The winter hadn't arrived but the chill was out. Asia looked and smile. She waved at the driver. She got in her car and unbuttoned her coat. The driver blew again. She looked at him and he got out the car.

Asia looked at him with his peanut butter leather coat matching his peanut butter Timberlands. Asia nodded her head thinking to herself, "The hazel-eyed Haitian."

Asia stepped out the car. He reached out to her and she embraced his slender frame. Asia tapped on his car, "I see you still riding around in the bat mobile."

"You got jokes." Gavin smiled, "Write down your number so I can call you later."

"What Tara gone have to say about you calling me?" Asia asked sarcastically.

"I really don't care. What Tara don't know, won't hurt her. Besides, me and Tara not together right now."

"Yeah right, Gavin. She just had a baby." Asia poked out her lips.

"Has anyone ever told you that your lips look like a heart?"

"You are switching the subject?" Asia wrote the number down and got in her car.

She took the medicine to Aaron. She decided to stay awhile. Mr. Townsend had just brought Mrs. Townsend home from the hospital. Asia admired Mr. Townsend. He had fathered two boys that favored him. It looks like Mrs. Townsend just carried them. Her skin was pale and she resembled Tisha Campbell with Rhiana's forehead. She was going to have to undergo chemotherapy. After two hours, Asia said her good-byes and the Townsend's let her know she could stop by more often.

Asia walked in the door. She looked at Keith and Tyrone while shaking her head with disgust. They were watching television like zombies. She walked in the kitchen and Robert sat there looking like he had something to say and he did, "Wanda left."

"Where did she go?" Asia asked.

"She didn't say. She just left this note." he handed the note to Asia.

Robert,

This morning I watched the Color Purple. In all the times, I have watched that movie I never felt the way I feel today. I gave up my life for you. You allowed your sister to treat me as if I were trash. Then you allow her to do the same with her very own child. If you look into your Bible, become very familiar with Paul. He was locked up and never did he complain about the people who locked him up. He decided to do better once he became free.

All these years, I felt like you have treated me the same way Mister treated his wife. I feel as though I have been locked up. I can't take this abuse anymore. I believed you poisoned my boys and I can't stay here and wait on you to poison me. Tell Asia I'm sorry. I'm taking my fat ass somewhere to lose weight. See you in the afterlife because now I am free.

Wanda

Asia went straight to her room. She sensed something wasn't right. *"Tell Asia I'm sorry"* played over constantly in her mind. She knew exactly what sorry meant.

When she made it to her stash, she was glad to find that Wanda had only taken one shoebox. She didn't take the three fullest ones. Asia thought she probably had around five grand in the box that she took off with. Asia would have given her more if she would have asked. If she knew she wanted to leave, she would have helped her out a long time ago. She was the closest thing to a mother Asia ever had.

The phone rang and rang. She knew her uncle wasn't about to answer it. She looked at her uncle and picked up the phone.

"Asia, what you doing?"

"Nothing, Shante."

"Guess what I bought you?" the excitement could be heard through the phone.

"What?" Asia asked as she flipped her eyelids.

"Come to the door." Shante stood holding Asia's new cell phone. Her job had come up with company incentives. Discounted cell phone plans were something she and her friend could use.

Asia hung up the phone. She looked at Keith and Tyrone and rolled her eyes. She opened the door and there stood Shante with her new friend, a Nokia cell phone.

Shante came through the door and followed Asia to her room.

"Hey Uncle Rob." Shante spoke while passing him in the kitchen.

"What's wrong with him?" Shante shut Asia's door.

"Wanda left." Asia said as she looked through her closet.

"I would have left his ass a long time ago. He mentally

abused her. Then had the nerve to be fucking with other women." Shante said aggressively.

"Well that's they business. Guess who I'm about to hook up with?"

Shante hated to say it, but her friend had become a whore. She worked every day to get what she wanted and Asia lay on her back getting more. She couldn't complain because her friend was generous.

Asia walked Shante to the door. When she got to the door, Gavin was already outside.

"I see he ain't rolling in the bat mobile anymore." Shante looked at Asia.

"He is doing it big in his blue BMW, huh." Asia snuggled in her burgundy leather jacket and clicked clacked down the steps as she strutted to his car in her burgundy Nine West three quarter length boots.

"What year is this?" Asia got in the car.

"It's a '96." Gavin pulled off before she could shut the door.

Shante walked on home shaking her head.

Gavin and Asia pulled in the parking lot of the AMC. He went forty-five minutes out the way to go to the movies. Few blacks frequented the south county area in St. Louis. After seeing the movie *Belly,* Gavin took her back home.

The sun was in the west when he came to pick her up the next day. She was glad he came back in the BMW. She liked the way the car drove. It was a smooth ride.

"Where we going today?" Asia asked.

"Where you wanna go?" Gavin looked over at Asia as he hopped on highway 70 going west.

"It really doesn't matter. I'm just here for the ride."

The car ride was an hour long. He pulled up in the Saint Peter Townhouses. Gavin opened the door and Asia just sat there.

"Are you going to get out?" Gavin looked at Asia.

"I didn't think you wanted me to come with you because you didn't say anything when you were getting out the car."

"Asia, how old are you?" Gavin asked.

"I'm eighteen. Why?" Asia stated with a slight attitude.

"When your birthday?"

"May fifteenth. Why you want to know?"

"The Taurus. The bull." Gavin opened the door, "I'm a Capricorn."

The apartment was fully furnished. The green sofa was plush. He took Asia's leather jacket and hung it up in the closet. He hung his black leather jacket on the back of the dining room chair that sat in the dining area.

Asia sat on the sofa and the softness embraced her body. Gavin cut on the big screen television. Moments later, he had released himself from his black jogging pants. Asia looked at all that shaft. All the penises she had seen, she had never seen one that was not circumcised. The skin hung, making his ten inches look twelve.

Asia stood in front of him and undressed. While taking off a one piece of clothing at a time, he signaled her to come closer to the sofa. She was about to straddle him and he instructed differently. She was now squatting over his face as her clitoris was being tickled by his nose. The feeling of his tongue he was giving, was nothing like when Brandon visited down south. When he felt her legs trembling, he brought her down to lie on the floor. He was struggling with placing on the plastic and her love box was anticipating his arrival. When he went in, she let out a loud sigh. R. Kelly sang about the Greatest Sex and that's what Gavin had given Asia, the greatest while that Capricorn dwelled inside the walls of that Taurus.

Gavin was constantly on her mind. She couldn't wait until he came from the Ram's game. Asia thought she'd give Andre a call. She needed to her his voice. When he said he was mad because this was going to be the first Thanksgiving away from his family, Asia asked him did he want to come home. She could buy him a bus ticket. She didn't feel safe putting her car on the highway. He said it was fine. He was going to have dinner with his roommate's family. Asia looked at her cell phone and saw that Gavin was calling.

She clicked over and told him she would call him right back. He let her know he would just call when he get outside.

"Who won?" Asia asked when she got in the car.
"New Orleans Saints."

The drive was quiet. Gavin went to every hotel in the

city of St. Louis. There was no hotel with any vacancies. Due to the Rams and Saints game, the hotels and motels were packed.

"Why we can't go to the first place we went to." Asia asked.

"I moved my stuff out. Tara and I were getting back together so we moved into a new apartment. I had to put her out. She keeps stealing." Gavin looked straight into traffic.

Asia knew about Tara. She never asked any questions. Gavin was hitting her off with cash, so she sat there wondering why Tara had to steal from him. Asia had never asked him for anything, he just gave it to her. In the little time, he had replaced the money Wanda had stolen.

Gavin pulled up to Westminster Place apartments.
"I stay on the next block over. Now you need a key to open up the door to get into the apartment building. Go through the back door and you can walk right up to it. I took the key from Tara. She can only get in the back door. Now she is supposed to be at her mother's house. You don't have to go if you don't want to. We can hook up another day."
"I'll go." Asia followed him through the side of the apartment complex.
The door slammed behind them. Gavin turned to make sure it was locked. Asia looked around. There were four doors, two on each side of the stairway. They walked back to the last door on the right side. Once inside, Gavin put up a four by four that blocked the door.
She sat on the same green sofa that was at the other apartment. She watched as he maneuvered the four by four between the back door and the cabinet.

He walked toward the back. He reentered the room with some comforters and pillows. Gavin made a pallet on the floor in front of the sofa. Asia lay on the pallet getting butterflies. She couldn't enjoy the caressing and the affection Gavin was putting down. He fell asleep when he was finally done. Asia didn't sleep at all.

Gavin looked at her and could tell she was nervous. She went to shower and he went to get the car. Asia heard a sudden noise and she cut the water off. Someone was trying to get in the back door. She dressed quickly, ran to the front of the apartment and stared at both doors. The front door opened as the back door was being kicked. Gavin looked at her and he went to the back door. Asia sat on the sofa grabbing a pillow off the floor. The butterflies came back. She sat and watched Gavin as he braced himself between the lower cabinet and the back door. The door was being kick so hard the sunlight was coming through the cracks.

Suddenly the kicking had come to an end. Asia wondered how long Gavin was going to be able to hold that door. He was really using all that strength in his legs. Then there was a knock. Gavin looked through the peephole.

"This Darnell." Gavin said to Asia.

"The dude that use to be with Dillian?"

"Yeah." Gavin whispered.

"What he doing over here?" Asia was trying to figure out why she just didn't run out the door Gavin had just come in.

"He and his gal stay two buildings down." Gavin opened the door.

Darnell looked directly at Asia. He didn't move to come in. He stood there as if he was staring at the door, "Man

I knew you were in here. Tara was kicking the shit out that door."

"Does she think I'm in here?"

"Nope. She thinks you got something up to the door. She said she just want to get the rest of her stuff. What you doing with her?"

Gavin looked back at Asia. She was holding on to that pillow for dear life. She wasn't afraid of Tara. She was afraid of the fact that Tara knew her and she knew Andre.

Darnell told Gavin he would talk to Tara for ten minutes. That would give him time to get out the apartment. Gavin watched as Darnell walked down the sidewalk. Darnell gave him thumbs up.

The car ride was quiet. When Gavin started to apologize, Asia really didn't want to hear it. She looked out the window and vowed she would never enter anyone else's apartment.

As soon as she got out the car, she pulled her cell phone from out her jacket pocket. She had to tell Shante everything that just happened. Once they shared that laugh, she was okay.

As Asia walked on the porch, the ambulance pulled up. Uncle Rob opened the door before she grabbed the doorknob. Asia moved out of the paramedic's way. Seconds later, Tyrone was being brought out on a stretcher.

Asia felt no remorse. She remembered when Shante told her that Keith held her down making her suck his sex organ while Tyrone rammed his sex organ in her anal canal. "What away to lose your virginity." Asia thought.

They had tied her up for five hours to a concrete pole in a vacant building. She was forced to eat their feces. When she was done eating the feces, they pissed all over her. They had gone from turning flips to kidnapping Shante and holding her hostage. The thought of Shante being hurt had Asia furious.

Asia went to her little stash to put away the money Gavin had given her. She moved some stuff around and found the dope she had gotten from Fabian. She was wondering was it any good. She didn't know anybody she could give it to.

Uncle Rob called to ask her to feed Keith. She wanted him to starve, but she considered the fact the she knew Keith only did what Tyrone had told him to do. Asia's frustration was simply because he didn't have enough sense to disagree.

Asia decided to order Chinese. The best Chinese was Bing Lau on the corner of Grand and Sullivan Avenue. The drive wasn't far from the house. When she walked inside the Chinese Restaurant, it was filled to capacity. The spatulas and other cooking utensils squeaked with echoing sounds that could make the flesh crawl. She ordered her usual, a whole order of shrimp fried rice, with two grape Vess sodas.

"Your feet got to be tired." the individual with corn rolls and Cartier frames coming through the door said to Asia.

Asia looked down at her Manolo boots, "Why would you think that."

"Girl, cause you been running across my mind all day!" the braid boy and his entourage shared a laugh.

Asia rolled her eyes because that was the corniest thing she had ever heard. She didn't think it was funny even when the Fresh Prince said it. When she looked at him, he favored Will Smith with Jazzy Jeff's complexion.

Chapter 13

HEATH

"Why did you give me such a hard time when I met you at the Chinese joint?"

"That line you came at me with was so lame." Asia sat in the front of Heath's house picking and throwing pieces of grass to the sidewalk. She gazed at his brown skin and the prominent features of his eyes and nose. While occupying the top spot of the concrete step, Asia sat and looked at him wondering if the Cartier frames he was sporting were knock offs. All the time she spent surveying magazines looking to find out the all the styles and the names of the top of line items, she didn't take the time to familiarize herself with the authenticity of the item.

Heath walked from the steps and ran to the door of a black Grand Prix that pulled up. When Asia tried to hold a conversation with him, he turned to run back to the next car that pulled up.

The darkness was falling upon the night. The night air was fighting to surface. The wind didn't stop the action of the fiends as they rushed to be served. The hustlers were scrambling to serve the rush. Turn your head and you're liable to have to wait for the next go round. Down from the crowd sat Asia and Heath, as he watched the crowd making sure he wouldn't get skipped.

Heath's older cousin, Isaiah, had his soldiers out on his block serving his poison. It would be against Isaiah religion to take the risk of hustling a product that came with plenty of jail time. For his own selfish reasons, Isaiah didn't care who was risking their freedom as long as it wasn't him. He had done this all for the love of money.

Asia sat and watched as Heath and six other friends took turns running back and forth to the cars that rolled up. She had gotten tickled off when she watched the smallest and youngest guy, Lil Terrell, out on the block. He had gotten D-bowed out of his turn a few times. He made a bad choice when he confronted the dude that took his turn. It lead to a big embarrassment. Lil Terrell got slapped like a whore by her pimp for not having his money. Lil Terrell had several friends out there to speak up for him but he didn't need their assistance. He was the littlest thing out on the block equipped with the most heart. Terrell left and came back with his street sweeper.

The way he cleared the street, one could assume he was equipped with a street cleaner. The incident shut down the block for an hour. No one was hurt but the police came. As usual, no one had seen anything so the call was useless.

Asia had found a way to get rid of the dope she had hidden in her closet. She cracked a few jokes with Heath about being on the block so she could make her own money. He let her know it was cool and she could comp from his cousin. He was impressed when she told him she could get it herself.

The next day, Asia was out on the set getting her hustle on. She worked in Heath's spot. She was able to get her work off after every other sale he made. For the next five days, she was out on the block with Heath. His cousin felt he was out there parlaying and he didn't like it one bit.

Lil Terrell was out on a new set. Rumor had it he was able to work on the block, which he lived. Therefore, he was taking their customers. With the sales coming slow, Asia figured it wasn't worth it and it wasn't her dope in the first place. She cut a deal with Heath.

The deal was each twenty that he sold she just wanted five dollars. She wanted to give it to him but she figured she could make a small profit and that could be some money she could send it to Andre.

When she got into his bed that five went from everything that he sold that was hers, she got all the money for it. She gave him part of what he sold because he was doing all the work. When Heath's cousin, Isaiah, found out that Asia was now Heath's supplier, he wanted to know who supplied her.

Chapter 14

ISAIAH

"Hey Asia, why don't we put our money together and get a big eight?"

Asia looked at the six foot and three inch tall occupant that was occupying her space as she stood in line about to order her and Heath a value meal from Mc Donald's. Isaiah had caught her off guard. She had seen him on the block a few times but she had never heard his voice. She was wondering how he knew her name.

Heath had spoke about Isaiah and how he had everybody on the block hustling for him. Heath only participated because it put a couple of dollars in his pocket. He wasn't out there trying to make it a career. She stood in the line wondering why would this hustler who had a little drug empire going on, want to go half on anything with her.

"You take my money and when you get yo lil dope, get me some too." Isaiah was standing there looking like the devil he was.

She figured he was being sarcastic. Asia had no clue that she had a half of kilo of cocaine that had an estimated street value of fifty grand. Isaiah was not seeing this kind of money. When she brought him back, more dope than money he put in, he was trying to meet her connect. He felt that with the right connection, he could blow up major in the game.

Isaiah convinced Asia to stop coming around. His tongue was flooded with lies. Little did he know that she was just about out. The mentioning of the police watching had convinced her enough to stay away.

In small talk, Isaiah learned that Asia was a huge fan of Jamie Foxx. He and a few other comics were coming through the House of Comedy. He surprised Asia with the tickets and she was astonished with the fact her favorite celebrity was in her presence. Isaiah knew a couple of dudes that were working backstage. Asia was able to make her way backstage and take pictures with Jamie Foxx. Being star struck, she couldn't get a word out.

After the show, Isaiah took her out for a bite to eat. Culpepper's was his choice. Asia fell in love with the hot wings. The special sauce left Asia wanting more when she was done. Isaiah convinced Asia not to go home.

He pulled up to a familiar spot. Asia sat thinking that this wasn't a good idea. She was not trying to give anybody something to discuss. It was after twelve and she knew there was nothing going to be open, but her legs. She wanted to tell him to take her home, but she felt as though she didn't want to disappoint him, after all, he showed her such a nice time.

Asia walked inside the hotel room. The room smelled cheap. The draft wasn't helping. Isaiah walked over to the window unit to cut on the heat. Asia sat on the bed holding tightly to her coat.

"With a little of my love and affection it could warm you up." Isaiah removed his black hoodie.

Asia looked at him. She wanted to roll her eyes but she showed a little teeth. She was fighting with her thoughts. Telling herself if she would have just said she was ready to go home all this could have been avoided. Now she was sitting here thinking of Andre. "Bad things always seem to happen to decent people," is what she remembered hearing him say once. She began fighting with herself trying to determine her decency. Asia watched as Isaiah as he began to undress. She looked over at his darkness and couldn't happen to think to herself, "Not another six foot three and hung like a flea!"

Chapter 15

WILLIE

"Asia, you want to go up to the basketball tournament?" Shante held the phone waiting on her response. It had been a while since her and her friend had hung out. Her hours and job duties had increased. Shante knew that Asia probably wanted Andre in her company right now, but he wasn't coming home anytime soon.

"What tournament?" Asia asked.

"It's a high school tournament going down at Normandy High School. The different high schools are playing against each other in the tournament. They play to defeat one another and the top two schools face off. Something like that. I figure it will give us something to do." Shante shrugged her shoulders as if Asia could see her. Shante's younger sister was listening in. Now Shante's younger sister wanted to go. She never really had many chances to hang out with her older sister because majority of her time was always with Asia, if Shante wasn't working.

The crowd was wild. Cheerleaders were cheering and the bleachers were rocking. The basketball was constantly being slammed dunk. The gym was filled and as the game heated up, all the static was about to jump off with the referees. They were making one bad call after another. The referees probably couldn't believe that the spectators were not there acting a fool but enjoying the fruits of the game.

Asia made a connection with a player who had the body of L. L. Wherever he moved her eyes were on him. It was as if the gym was silent and Asia and the subject were the only ones in the room. When he winked, Asia turned to look to make sure he was winking at her. He dribbled and pointed in her direction. His teammate moved in the direction he pointed. He was so busy looking at Asia his opponent had stolen the ball.

"Jemez, get in the game!" the coach yelled from the sideline.

Shante chuckled seeing her friend in action. She excused herself so that she could release her bladder. On her back from the rest room, she was stopped in her tracks as this figure stood before her.

"Brown Suga tell me your name. I can't let you leave without getting your name and number." Shante smiled.

"Brown Suga fits you well, but I'd like to know that government name you go by."

Shante smiled again. She hadn't had time for dating. It really wasn't important. Keith and Tyrone had stolen the feeling from her years ago. She would occasionally talk to a few dudes but as soon as the conversation shifted to sex, the conversations were over.

"Shante." she blushed as she stated her name.

"Shante, I was about to make you miss the game, because I wasn't about to let you go without you telling me your name. Well Shante, I'm Willie."

"You know you look like..."

He cut her off, "Yeah, I know I look like that cat from Three Six, but all my shit is normal." He raised both of his hands.

They exchanged numbers and went on to watch the game. Shante's runway walk sent a jones through Willie's body.

Jack Frost was out and Asia was in. Since Shante had met Willie, their time together was at its ultimate low. Asia didn't trip because she was glad that Shante could finally found some companionship.

Sitting in her room, she laid fumbling through her new magazines. Uncle Rob found himself dealing with too much, so he placed his boys in a state facility. He was slowly decaying himself. Wanda had left and she didn't look back. Asia had right before her eyes, the saying: "you never miss what you had till it's gone." Robert didn't have to say a word, it showed.

Her cell phone rang. She tried to figure out who would be calling her. Shante was with Willie and usually Shante didn't call a lot when they were together. She had already talked to Andre and he was going somewhere with his roommate and he had gotten the money she had sent Western Union so she found it strange that her phone was ringing.

"Hello." Asia answered.

"May I speak to, Asia?" the male voice asked seductively.

"Speaking."

"Hey Asia, this is Jemez. The one you met at the basketball tournament."

"I know who Jemez is. I only met one." Asia giggled. Thinking how she and Shante had both met a someone.

"I know them cats were trying to get at you." Jemez stated.

Asia laughed thinking of her days in school and going to the games. She and Shante would walk around to in search of anyone's attention. Their strut flaunted their five star chic status. This time she wasn't guilty of that. She sat and actually watched the game. She just found something that caught her attention. She was surprise herself when she walked up to him and gave him her number. She was the one always being approached.

"What you getting into?" He asked.

"Jemez, I'm not getting into anything. I am trying to stay out the cold."

"You want some company?"

Asia didn't know she had met the most aggressive person who was younger than she was. She thought about the idea of him keeping her company. It did help that he had the ultimate body and he favored her favorite celebrity. She had never had company other than Andre and Shante in her home.

She didn't even know if her uncle would allow the company of a new male in his home. Today was not the day she was going to find out. Besides she and Robert never said much to each other anymore. He would let her know when he was hungry and let her know when he was about to visit the home.

He was slowly and slowly deteriorating. He never had company. His friend who owned the building had slowed up on his visits, so Asia didn't know where to begin to ask about company. She just thought she could tell Jemez just to come over.

"You know Jemez I am going to have to take a rain check. I am lying in my bed and I really don't feel like getting up."

"I can lay with you." he was not about to give up that easy.

"What?"

"Well Asia, you opened that door."

"Well I'm closing it."

"It's all good! That's cool." Jemez started to laugh.

Chapter 16

KHALIL

"What's on the agenda for today?" Shante looked over at her friend, wishing she would come back to planet Earth.

Asia sighed and looked at Shante, wishing she could save her from the feelings she was undergoing. Asia couldn't believe that Andre had not tried to call her once. She thought about getting in her car; going to his house and make him listen to what she had to say. However, she thought against it. She knew that once Andre was mad, he needed to be the one to come around with the truce. Besides, he was armed and she didn't want him to have to use his weapon if she was caught on his premises. She finally decided to answer Shante. She was sitting there patiently.

"What are your plans?" Asia moped.

"Well, I was going to ride down on Willie and gun his ass down once he walked out the door." Shante said without a smirk.

Asia laughed. Shante was shocked to see the smile. It was almost like the look everybody gave Sophia when she was letting everyone know that she was home.

"Let's go! I got to get out this house." Asia walked out the door.

Shante was out for blood. Shante drove down a familiar street. This happened to be the street that Asia met Khalil on when she was with Jemez.

######

"What is a tight young thing doing with this young hoop star?" Asia looked around as she couldn't believe that this dude had these type of balls. She looked at Jemez and he didn't say a word. He looked straight ahead as if he hadn't seen this dude walk up to his car. Asia didn't know what to say but instructed Jemez to take her home. She didn't know if this was a game that they played or if Khalil was openly disrespecting Jemez.

Asia had never felt this awkward. Khalil was a lot taller than Jemez but Jemez was all muscle. The hoop star had a body and she was hoping he wasn't letting all this masculinity go to waste. This wasn't the aggressive lil dude she shared telephone conversations with. The confirmation of his aggressiveness was shown the moment he had her in his bed. Now he was sitting there like nothing was going on. Asia was pissed when she told him to take her home and he still hadn't made a move.

Khalil dropped a hundred dollar bill in her lap and told her to catch a cab.

Money made Asia moist just from the sight of it. Asia would make it her business to become very familiar with Khalil.

After the cab took Asia home, she would sporadically take, trips to see if she would see Khalil standing outside. She finally saw him and she stopped to talk. He bent her over a couple of times and he paid dearly for that piece of ass.

######

Shante pulled up on the parking lot of the Royal Palace.

The Royal Palace is a hole in the wall, local lounge found in the hood. The DJ kept it crunk. It drew all kinds of crowds. The drinks were watered down but the people were there to party. There was not a night that the place wasn't packed. Asia sat in silence because she knew what they were there for.

Chapter 17

LORENZO

Shante was driving to an unknown destination. She halted at a red light. The car ride was silent. Asia looked to her right and Lorenzo was sitting at the light right next to them. Asia looked over at him. She sat staring waiting on him to look over and notice her. Before the light was about to change he put down what he had in his hand, looked over, and noticed a familiar face. She waved and he waved back. He was about to roll down the window and say his peace, but when the light turned green Shante just drove off.

It seemed like it was just yesterday when Asia was kicking it with Lorenzo. She met him at North Oaks bowling alley when she was hanging out with Willie and Shante one night. He was there flossing with his friends Mario and Quincy.

Asia was standing at the concession stand when she felt the hardness of a man pressing up against her buttocks. She turned around to what could have been a Chris Brown impersonator. She giggled at him. She looked him over with no interest. Not having anything against the light skin brother, she just preferred Hershey's chocolate any day.

When his friends started to joke about light skin not being in, and Lorenzo would come back with, "We ain't ever left."

Asia smiled, but when he pulled out the knot to pay for

his ordered, she creamed. She couldn't argue whether or not light skin was in or out, but she knew one thing for sure, green was definitely in. She bowled even though she didn't know how. Shante wasn't any competition, either. She was just there because it was something Willie like doing. The lanes were filled. The sound of bowling pins trampling the alleys was drowning out a few conversations. Music was coming over the speaker, but it could barely be heard. Asia was just enjoying being with her friend. Lorenzo and his crew were down three lanes from them. Just as he was watching her caramel swagger, she was checking him out.

Lorenzo occupied a spot over on St. Louis City's south side. The apartment was small but nicely decorated. There was nothing extravagant about the apartment. It presented a sense of comfortableness in all the plainness that she noticed. Everything came from Ashley furniture. Either he just got it or he wanted everyone to know that he shopped at Ashley's because the tags were still on the furniture.

"You know this looks very tacky." Asia looked at Lorenzo.

He had no clue as to what she was talking about as he asked, "What?"

"These damn tags. You need to take this mess off. You must think your furniture is just like that baseball cap because you haven't taken the tags off."

Lorenzo pulled his fitted cap off and looked under it, "Girl this authenticates this joint. If the tags are bothering you pull them off."

That was all she needed to hear. She walked around the entire apartment with a small grocery bag removing the tags and placing them in the bag. She had been kicking it with him for a minute. She was getting use to the fact he had his own spot and the only pop ups that came were his comrades, Mario and Quincy. If she hadn't known any better, one would have thought they stayed there. They stopped by often no matter the time.

Every time Quincy came around, Asia had this peculiar feeling that tingle her spine. He would look at her as if he were undressing her with his eyeballs. She liked her men chocolate but Quincy was beyond chocolate. He was as dark as a burnt crispy piece of barbecue. Quincy's stare was demonic. It didn't help that part of his eyes that should have been white had a red pinkish filmy looking tint. The pinkish matched the thick pink lips that hung profusely from his face. His nostrils were wide as a raging bull.

Asia was starting to question her skills. It had been two weeks of sexing going down and Lorenzo still hadn't kicked her down with any dough. He fed her every now and then. She had to let him know that she wasn't Betty Crocker and she wasn't about to cook anything. He complained about her not cooking, although he didn't mind having her around.

Lorenzo was having a little gathering at his spot so the guys could watch the Nuggets and the Celtics play. That's when Asia discovered the secret. She realized that her skills were still intact. It was just that she was playing house with the wrong one. Mario was the man she needed to get at. Get at was just what she was about to do. She wanted to kick herself for wasting her time with Lorenzo. She didn't believe that her K-9 senses had failed her. All this time she was around him, she hadn't noticed anything. Eavesdropping on a few conversations, she realized that Mario had put Lorenzo up in this spot. Mario wanted to complain about Asia spending so much time there, but he had his own intentions.

Asia knew that the mandatory time wasting needed to come to a halt. She still had some dough stashed, but it was getting low. She had taken care of Andre and did some much needed shopping. The things that were in her closet were becoming old and some new fashions had come on the scene. She liked to set trends, but trendsetting was not going to pop off in her old gear. Her wasting time with Lorenzo, was putting a dent in her cash flow. It was time to replenish her cash flow and she had just laid eyes on the individual that was about to donate to her benevolent fund.

When Mario entered, she made every indication that she wanted him. The hip hugger Parsucco jeans and the tightly fitted shirt only increased her chances. She was bending her frame in every way, as she would sit down everything from coasters to napkins throughout the room. Mario smiled to let her know that she had his attention and had him at attention.

Chapter 18

MARIO

"What's up with you and my boy?" Mario looked every bit like E-40 and Asia was going to see if he was sick with the cash flow *In A Major Way*.

"You want me to call Lorenzo and let him know you waiting on him to come back?" Asia was pulling his hoe cord. She already knew what Mario was there for. She was just playing his game. When she found out that Mario was the man, she started paying attention to every conversation that was taking place. She already knew that Mario had sent Lorenzo on a blank mission so that he could get a little sample of some Asia. She just couldn't understand why a dude of his caliber was playing a game just to get some. She was wondering about his mandatory time wasting as he was asking about them when it was really about her. She had wasted enough time and she was not about to waste anymore.

"So what's good? How much you are you willing to spend?" Asia cut right to the point.

He looked at Asia. He was kicking himself, had he know it was that easy, he would have kicked her down with a little dough a long time ago. He smiled asking, "Spend on what?"

Asia dropped the robbed that she was wearing. Her caramel skin glistened and Mario was about to bust. He couldn't believe what he was witnessing. The vagina was trimmed up nicely looking like a runaway. She walked over, stood on the couch, and put it all up in his face. She taunted him as he was trying to taste her.

"You never said how much you were spending." Asia thought she had lost it. She never had to ask for money and she hadn't reached the point of working for it until now. She thought he had come prepared because she noticed that on Wednesdays, Lorenzo got off. She soon found out that Wednesday was her payday as well. Mario reached for his back pocket and threw five grand on the table. Asia looked at the cash. Without any shame in her game, Asia went straight to work. She was surprised to see fat boy pull out all of every bit of eight inches of thickness. He put in work on his boy's woman, right on his brand new burgundy leather Ashley couch he helped him get.

All good things must come to an end. Mario had to go off and run his mouth. Now Quincy wanted his piece of the action. He threatened that if she wasn't going to break him off with the good stuff, he was going to tell Lorenzo. Asia agreed, but there was only one problem; Mario didn't state the facts; in a month's time, he had tricked off twenty grand.

Now, either Quincy needed to present half of that twenty grand or he wasn't coming close to the performance Mario had received. Now she got down, but it was her choice of whom she got down with. She knew he probably would come up empty handed and that would be effortless for her to tell him no. She couldn't even bring herself to stomach his touch.

Quincy was about to knock her down and take what he wanted. Asia could see the wickedness in his eyes. She stood ready to take him on. He didn't realize she was a force to be reckoned with. He had her with her back against the wall and she wasn't about to fight him off. She just knew that when it was all over, Quincy would regret that he'd ever wanted that piece of ass. Lorenzo came through the door.

Asia knew that he should be walking through the door any minute now because he had only stepped out to get them a bite to eat. Lorenzo didn't ask any questions. All he saw was his boy backing Asia in a corner. He couldn't tell if Asia's face was showing fear. It appeared to Lorenzo that Asia was enticing Quincy. Lorenzo was having mixed emotions because the enticing look also seemed immoral.

Quincy didn't see it coming. Lorenzo hit his ass so hard that Quincy stumbled into Asia making her fall to the floor. Asia knew that this could no longer go on and she was done playing with fire. Lorenzo was showing too many emotions for her. She walked away, not looking back. He didn't let her go without blowing up her phone, but he eventually got the picture and stopped calling.

Chapter 19

NE'QUAN

Asia sat in the car. She was trying to think about just what they were going to do. She wanted to make him suffer for hurting her friend the way he did. Now she was dealing with her own situation but she felt that what was meant to be would be. When he called and just held the phone, she figured that he just needed some more time.

Shante was on point. She was watching everything that was moving on the parking lot. She knew when the club had reached its maximum amount. Nothing was distracting her from watching what was going in and what was coming out of the Royal Palace door tonight. She could even tell who was sneaking drinks in the club because she was watching the door like a hawk.

"Asia, what's his name right there?" Shante pointed to the bald fella coming out of the door.

"Girl, that's Ne'quan, B.K.A. Slick Rick." Asia smiled.

"Remember when we met his ass at that concert when Jay-Z was here. That was the first dude I saw with some platinum." Shante chuckled.

Asia was tickled to death, "Yo slow ass talking about why that dude got on all that silver jewelry. Now you trying to act like you knew he had on a platinum chain!"

Shante looked at Asia and laughed. She knew Asia was up on all the new fads. She didn't know what the hell platinum was. She just thought it was silver.

Asia thoughts took her elsewhere.

"What you about to get in once you leave here?" Asia asked as Ne'quan approached the car.

"I'm about to go home and get in my bed." Ne'quan smiled. He had just been released from doing a six-year bid. His first day out, his boys had taken him to a concert that he didn't want to attend. He wanted some time alone. His woman had moved on during his incarceration. Now his boys had him in this club surrounded by more people.

He was ready to go home.   One of his boys took care of his house while he was on his extended vacation. In his face was some potential ass. He didn't want to run it away. She was decent looking and nicely dressed in her DKNY attire. He wanted to ask her could he get into her since she wanted to know so much.

"Shante, I'm about to leave with the silver chain. I'll call you as soon as we get where we are going." Asia walked away.

Shante wanted to say something to her friend. She didn't want to appear as though she was judging her but; she felt the need to tell her that she didn't have to go to bed with every person she met. She wanted to bring Andre up, but she didn't want to piss her off. Asia had a way of taking most things the wrong way.

Asia walked outside the club, following two dudes and Ne'quan to a blue BMW. Ne'quan let them know that he was about to drop them off before they exited the club.

Ne'quan looked at Asia, "Do you remember me from the fifth grade?"

Asia looked at him for a long time. "Hell naw! You use to be dirty as hell! You wore a *Start a New Day* tee shirt every day." Asia laughed.

"Yeah, I'm nigga rich now." Ne'quan rubbed his chin.

In between dropping his friends off, they had small talk about some of the people they knew. He even talked about a couple people Asia use to date. He made her think about Ethan, Fabian, Gavin, and Heath. Ne'quan didn't remember seeing Asia with any of them; he just talked about dudes he knew that was getting money. That entire night consisted of him reminiscing about being in the street. He had mentioned this chic in his conversation a couple times. So Asia wanted to know why did this chic leave him for dead when he was down.

He went into this long drawn out story about how he took her to Miami to propose to her. On the day they came back to St. Louis and made it home, he was so hungry that he sent her to get pizza. When she went in to order the pizza, she was kidnapped. He was so animated when he said, "These niggas followed him all the way from Miami, Florida to kidnap my gal."

He talked about how he was down there splurging. When these gentlemen saw his presidential Rolex, they were on him. He said all he kept saying was, "This how we do it in the Lou." Asia wanted badly to ask, "Why didn't they just get yo ass when you were in Miami"? He must have been reading her mind cause as she thought it, he came out saying, "The only reason they didn't get me down there, cause they knew my money was back home."

Asia was done. She was not about to waste any more time with him. In between conversations, she went to the bathroom. That was only done because the moment he wanted to run up in it, she was going to tell him that she just came on. She lived by condoms. No one was about to get it raw, but she knew the moment she told him that she didn't have any he would come out of nowhere with plenty.

Ne'quan talked her to sleep. He went on with so many stories that Asia start calling him Slick Rick. The morning couldn't come fast enough. As soon as Asia saw the sun, she called Shante. When Shante came, he wanted to go to breakfast.

When they arrived at Denny's, he started stating about how he was locked up. He had just made some type of move. The dude he made the move with got caught up as soon as he left him. So he sent the police back to him and that's when the girl he was with said that was enough.

Asia looked at him and wanted to just bust him out. She decided she would let him shine in his own glory because that would be the last time she would ever see his stunting ass.

On their ride home, Shante said to Asia, "You know that stuff he was talking about, I read it in some book. That's when Asia let her know that's why she had been calling him Slick Rick, the storyteller.

A week later Asia and Shante saw Slick Rick at Red Lobster on St. Charles Rock Road. He was with a girl who looked like she had missed many meals. Her blonde weave was scraggly and her clothes appeared dingy. He was wearing the same Roc-A-Wear gear he had on at the concert. He came over to the table to speak. He wanted to know why he had never heard from Asia anymore. He didn't have a number or any way of contacting her. Asia let him know that they had gotten off to a bad start and maybe he needed some time to adjust to the streets.

He wanted to clown Asia right at that moment. He couldn't understand that stunting might have been the game when he went in, but when he got out, Asia was not the one to fall for it.

Chapter 20

OMARI

Asia's phone began to vibrate. She couldn't remember when she put her phone on vibrate. She pulled her cell phone from her side. The screen read Shannon.

"Hello." Asia listened for the caller to respond.

"What's up Asia?" Shannon smacked on a piece of chewing gum.

"Nothing, what's up with you?" Asia looked at Shante. Shante was looking at Asia while waiting for her to announce the name of the caller. Asia slowly moved her lips whispering Shannon's name. Shante shook her head no. She knew Shannon or her mother wanted her to do something for them and today wasn't the day to be playing Captain Save-A-Hoe.

"Have you seen my sister? Momma said she has being calling her and calling her. She hasn't answered nan call. Momma said that's not like her. If she missed a call she would at least call back." Shannon waited on Asia to respond.

Asia looked over at Shante, "No I haven't seen Shante. I talked to her early. She was going somewhere with Willie."

Shante looked at Asia and rolled her eyes. She placed her hands over her face thinking to herself, "Why didn't Asia come up with something better?" Shannon knew that she had seen Willie at the clinic with his children.

"Did his punk ass explain those damn kids that Shante seen him at the clinic with?" Shannon popped her gum as if she meant business.

"Shante got that all under control. He trunk tight, I mean she's trump tight." Asia laughed.

Shannon looked very strange at the receiver, "What you playing cards or something?"

Asia realized that she had been on the phone with Shannon too long. "Shannon I'll hit you back. If I talk to Shante, I will let her know that you all are looking for her."

Shannon let out a medieval outburst, "You do that!"

Shante glimpsed at Asia, "What was all that about? You laughing and shit, wanting to crack jokes. I don't see a damn thing that's funny!"

"You want to talk about funny. I left Omari off my list. How could I forget about him? You know I seen him on Martin Lawrence First Amendment comedy show."

Shante laughed thinking about Omari, "I heard he moved out to DC after he left LA.'

"How you hear about all that and I didn't?" Asia stared at Shante waiting on an answer.

"Girl, you know that girl, Natalie, that works with me, that is his cousin. Every time he did a comedy show somewhere, she comes in to work bragging. She was the one that gave me the tickets to the comedy show at the House of Comedy."

Asia and Shante stood looking for seats. Natalie happened to turn around and saw them standing in the door. She had saved them some seats right up front. She waved her hand but Shante had already spotted the bad weave when she walked through the door. She was hoping that Natalie saw her and invited her over. She didn't want to walk up to the front and get embarrassed.

Asia had her eyes on Omari when she walked through the door. He was neatly dressed in a pressed short sleeve blue oxford, light blue denim jeans and brown leather Diesel casual shoes. His stand was so sexy. He look like he was about to walk the runway and pose in some Sean John boxer's.

"I met this girl the other day and I told her a little lie." Omari put his pointer finger and thumb together to show as he laughed a little, "Now I got her wide open." He began to grind his body, "I am all up in it and she's screaming fuck me harder go deeper. Daddy you said you were going to give me ten inches. I told that bitch, I'm ma give ya five today and five tomorrow. That's my time I love y'all good night." The crowd roared with laughter. He had gotten a standing ovation. The crowd stood as Asia and Shante made it to their seats. Asia was relieved because she saw how the comedians would rip of the late comers. With them going to the front of the room, she didn't want to become a part of anyone's joke for the night.

The girls sat around a circular table that sat four. There was no one sitting next to Asia. Omari came over and sat right next to her, "Natalie, are you going to introduce me to your beautiful friends.

Before Natalie could speak, Asia had taken control of the conversation. She looked him directly in his light brown eyes, "That's just like a nigga. You sitting right next to me and got the nerve to look right over me and ask somebody about me and my friend." Asia shook her head.

Omari laughed. He rubbed his smooth coal black hair. His short hair was manicured neatly to his scalp. He looked Asia in her eyes, "You got jokes. That's all right. We are going to be back on top real soon."

Everyone at the table shared a laugh. The night went on. They listened to at least ten more comedians. Asia watched as these people chased their dreams. She couldn't help but to think what would happen if she began to chase her dreams of being a well-known fashion designer. Asia and Shante happened to attend the comedy show on a night that the comedians were auditioning to be on Puff's Bad Boy of Comedy. After the show ended, Omari asked the women if they wanted to hit some clubs up on the eastside. It is just 2 minutes across the bridge. Asia wanted to go and hang out with him but she thought about it for the first time. This was the first real job she had. Andre's father pulled a couple of strings to get her on and she didn't want to mess up anything. Asia and Omari exchanged numbers.

"I'll call you tomorrow and maybe we can do lunch." Omari held the car door, waiting on Asia to let him know that it was okay for him to call her.

Shante sat laughing. Omari was looking like he did not want to go home. She looked over at Asia's blouse and her cleavage was looking very scrumptious. The way Asia exposed herself, Shante knew Asia had Omari's full attention. Then she looked back at Omari and the look in his eyes was telling Shante he thought the breast was scrumptious as well.

"I hate we missed the beginning of your set. You seemed to be pretty funny. The crowd loved you.' Asia made small talk. She was trying to cut him some slack and let him know everything was all-good.

Shante became impatient, "Omari, she will call you tomorrow. We have jobs we have to wake up and go to." Shante was glad to say that her dear friend had finally found work.

Asia was running a few police record checks. She was looking back and forth from her watch to the clock that was on the office wall. She was not going to be late like Cinderella about to miss the clock as it was about to strike twelve. She couldn't wait any longer. She wanted to be sitting down about to eat lunch by at least twelve thirty. She picked up her cell phone. She dialed and he instantly answered the phone. All she could hear was laughter. She waited to see if anyone was going to say anything. She couldn't hear anyone saying anything. All she could hear was someone mumbling and then some more laughter. Asia hung up the phone.

Omari looked at his phone. He had been pulling his phone from his clip checking to see if Asia had called him yet. He pulled his phone out and looked at the screen. The screen was flashing with the words displaying call end with forty-six seconds on it and Asia's name above it all. He called her right back.

Asia looked at the phone as it vibrated. She was hesitant before she answered. She was having second thoughts about going out with him.

"Hello."

"Asia, I am sorry I missed your call."

Asia responded nonchalantly, "You sounded busy."

"No, I am not busy. I was downtown meeting with some other comedians. We are talking about going on a road trip. They have competitions going on in several cities. So we are going to hit the road and go compete." Omari began to walk away from the group of people he was meeting with.

"Are you downtown right now?" Asia inquired.

"Yeah. I am downtown. Why you ask?"

"I work downtown and maybe we could do that lunch you were talking about last night." Asia grabbed her purse as she prepared to tell him where he was about to meet her.

"You work downtown. What kind of work do you do?" Omari was making small talk.

"I work at the police station." Asia grinned.

"The police station?" Omari smiled, "Are you serious?"

"Yes, I am serious. I have a civilian job. I basically run record checks."

"Can you delete my warrants out the system?" Omari turned to his group of friends, "Y'all want me to get all y'all warrants deleted so y'all want get locked up when we get on the road? I got the hook up at the police station." Omari smiled.

"I see you got jokes. You need to stop playing. I can't delete shit." Asia laughed, "How close are you to Union Station?"

"I am standing right outside Union Station." Omari looked at the Romanesque exterior of the building.

"Standing outside where, boy. I am about to meet you so that we can have lunch."

"I am standing right in front of the Hyatt Regency."

"Give me a few minutes and I'll be down there."

Asia received a ride from one of the officers. Omari watched as Asia exited the police cruiser. Omari looked at her heart shaped lips piercing tightly together as she smiled. Her perfectly arched eyebrows made her eyes appear to be seductive without her even saying one word.

Asia strutted over to him. She strutted in her black leather Empire pumps as if her name should have been on them instead of Jimmy Choo. The pleated stretched charmeuse BCBG Blouse had her breast looking more scrumptious than they did last night. Omari smiled as she approached him with mere confidence. Asia smiled right back at him.

"Why don't we go to Caleco's? It's nothing in here I want to eat for real." Omari nodded toward Union Station.

"What's at Caleco's that's so special?" Asia was trying to think of the menu. She had only been a couple of times herself, but it wasn't anything she had to frequent. She couldn't remember what she had on the few occasions that she did eat there.

"Girl they got the best veal. The veal is thinly sliced with mushrooms, tomatoes, and green bell peppers and its sautéed in this good tasting wine sauce."

Asia looked at him. She wanted to scream at him asking him, "Nigga, veal, what about some damn chicken?" She agreed.

Omari flagged the taxi. The restaurant was in walking

distance but he didn't know how long Asia had for lunch. Asia entered the cab. They pulled up in front of the restaurant in three minutes flat. Omari emerged from left side of the taxi. He walked around to the other side and open Asia's door. Asia smiled as she exited the car.

Omari ordered his veal and Asia chose the Chicken Fajita Salad. Asia was way past her lunch hour. It didn't matter to her. She never left the building that often to go to lunch anyway. She managed to befriend several individuals in her workplace so everything was cool for her. After lunch, they made plans to hook up together later on that day. Asia watched as Omari exited the building. She stood up once he entered into the taxi. Asia walked out the door. She was about to take her taxi back to the station.

A full size champagne Ford Crown Victoria pulled in front, on where she was standing.

"You could have taken me to lunch?" Andre smiled, "Are you on your way back to the station? Or are you standing here waiting on Shante?'

Asia walked over to the car and opened the door, "Are you following me?" she smiled, but the statement she made was very serious.

"I am coming from court. One the homicide cases I was on went to trial."

"You testified today?" Asia asked. She was thinking that she needed to either stop trying to be a playa or find out Andre's schedule before she called herself creeping.

"I didn't testify. I just wanted to know the outcome." Andre pulled in front of the station. Together they exited the car. Asia was glad the ride was over. She didn't want to know anything he was involved in. Besides, she had just had lunch with Omari and she didn't want Andre asking her anything about lunch.

Asia asked him what he was doing after work. She

needed to know because she had plans to see Omari. She was not about to let Andre throw a monkey wrench in her plans. He was going to shoot pool at some bar Darrell and Donald invited him to. Asia knew he didn't know how to shoot pool, so he had to be just going out for some beers.

Asia called Omari, "I am off work. So, where do you want me to meet you?"

"You can stop by over here." Omari smiled. He like the way Asia took charge.

"Stop over where?" Asia was thinking he was stupid. She started to tell him that she just met him yesterday and she doesn't know a damn thing about him and where he hung out.

"I thought when you got back to work that you ran my name and found out all about me. You chicks these days know y'all be doing background checks on niggas. Y'all be knowing our credit status and shit. Naw boo, you got a three seventy-five, call me when you get to seven hundred." Omari smiled at his own joke.

"You play too much." Asia laughed.

"I am over my mother's house. She stays on Kensington Avenue over here off Union. You can get it off Delmar."

Asia wanted to say you could get it all right. She giggled, "I need the address."

Omari gave her the address and she was on her way.

Asia pulled up directly in front the house. She called his phone to let him know that she was outside. He came to the door. He stood there as she exited her car. She strutted her way to the door. That runway walk turned Omari on.

Asia looked around. The house was enormous Victorian architecture. It was even decorated in a modern day Victorian décor. Asia noticed how immaculate his mother's home was.

"You live here?" Asia asked as she looked around. The pine-sol scent let her know that the entire house had to look this way.

"Why? Do you have a problem with a man that still lives at home with his mother?"

Asia glanced at his light brown eyes, "As long as you don't live in the basement."

Omari showed his pearly whites, "Now you have jokes I see. No, I don't live in the basement. My room is right upstairs, down the hall from my mom's room."

Asia looked intently at Omari, "Where is your mother now?"

"She and some of her friends took a trip to Hot Springs, Arkansas. They shopping and listening to some live entertainment and going to some type of resort. She's retired now and every since my father left she takes these trips. I think she got a lil tender or something because I don't ever see her when she leaves. I always see her when she comes back. She be having these facial expressions like she done hit the lottery or something."

Asia smiled as he talked about his mother. Her childhood memories started to surface. All she could see was the glare and the look of excitement that Omari had on his face when he spoke of his mother. She looked down, hating the fact that she couldn't tell a happy story about Janice.

Omari led her up the steps to his room. She was surprised. She thought she was about to see a kid's room with a grown man sleeping in it. It was more modern than the rest of the house. She could tell that it was decorated by his mother. Everything was Jacquard sage print. His king size bed had several different sized pillows; the curtains and throw rugs coordinated with the comforter. The room was so plush. The mattress felt like cotton candy. She knew she was lying on some top of the line items.

Asia looked down at her phone. She noticed that it was Omari calling her. She pressed ignore and place her phone back on her side.

"Dre, dinner was good. What made you think of this place?" Asia looked across the table at Andre. They were at a small bar and grill on the city's south side.

"Robinson put me on to this one day we went to lunch. I tasted the hot wings that they had here and I think they taste better than Culpeppers. I had to put you on it. So, what you think about the chicken?" Andre smiled and took a drink of his Apple Martini.

"The chicken was good, but you know Culpeppers just have this taste to me that can't be beat. I wish I knew the recipe that was in that sauce. I'll be slanging that sauce in the hood." Asia laughed.

The atmosphere was nice. Smooth jazz played throughout and flat screens were posted in areas where every customer could get a view of the screen. The crowd was diverse and the menu was exquisite. The hot wings were the appetizer that prepared you for an Italian cuisine. Asia was done with dinner once she got her phone call. She figured the night was young and Andre was probably going to check on his parents. Since he had been back home from school, his work schedule and parents had him preoccupied.

Andre licked his lips and smiled, "Did you want anything else to eat?"

Asia was already prepared to tell him she was good and was ready to go. She loved Andre, but other personalities amused her. Besides, she liked the attention that she would receive in a fresh relationship. "I can't eat another thing. You are interfering with my dime piece diet."

Andre stared at Asia and smiled, "Girl you are so silly. As much as you like to eat, I can't interfere with any type of diet you think you on. You need to be on a seafood diet. You see food and you eat it."

Asia's eyes took a circumference reaction to his comment, "Dre, that is so old and only so corny."

Andre chuckled as he excused himself to go to the restroom. Asia watched as he walked away. She pulled her phone from her side.

"Yeah what's up?" Asia asked.

"Yeah what's up? Damn, no how you doing. I am so sorry I missed your call." Omari waited on Asia to respond. Asia took a look back to the back of the room making sure Andre was not about to resurface as she spoke on her phone.

"Omari, I am sorry I missed your call. What are you up to?" Asia grinned.

"I was at the mall I wanted to know what your favorite color was. I was going to pick up something nice for you." Omari stood looking at the lingerie in Victoria Secret.

"What's your favorite color?" Asia had an idea of what he was trying to do. For the last two months, he was talking about getting her in some sexy lingerie, but Asia wasn't going for it. She realized she was doing a little too much going to his different comedy shows when Andre was somewhere watching the game. Then she realized that a game was coming on and Andre might watch it with his father.

"I'm a big fan of Prince. I liked him every since I was a child. I don't tell everybody that either." Omari ran his hands across a purple pair of panties.

"I guess you are trying to tell me that purple is your favorite color. So, since you like purple, you need to get what you like." Asia watched as Andre was about to make his way back to her.

"Well, once I leave the mall, why don't you meet me downtown, room three one four." Omari waited on her to respond.

"Three one four where?" Asia look at Andre as he took

his seat.

"314 is that club out there off of highway 270." Andre took his seat.

"The Omni Majestic Hotel.' Omari smiled.

"Alright." Asia placed her phone back on her hip.

Omari didn't know that was the end of the conversation. He hadn't given her the time. Then he had to make sure that he was going to get the hook up on the room number he had given her. His sister was working tonight and she was the hotel manager. If the room number changed, he would just call and let her know.

"What's popping off at 314?" Andre waited on Asia. He was hopping she was not about to ask him to go with her. He had already made plans to watch the game, the San Antonio Spurs against the Houston Rockets. The game was coming on at seven thirty and he planned to be in front of the television as soon as the game started.

"Shannon talking about her and a couple of her friends are going out there and she wanted me and Shante to come along. I have been out there a few times. The crowd is pretty much laid back. The grown and sexy is what I call it." Asia was hopping his was not about to ask her anymore questions that involved Shannon. She didn't want to continue to lie but if he asked, he was about to get a conversation full of lies. She was ready to go laugh at the silliness that Omari was bound to perform. It never failed. Asia was not a big fan of comedy, but the more she was around Omari, she was beginning to adore it. She wanted to take Andre to one of the shows, but she hadn't mentioned to Omari that she was involved with anyone. After each of his sets, he always made his way over to Asia's table and made himself comfortable. She was not about to put herself in any complicated situation. Andre would have to find comedy on his own.

"Are you going?" Andre needed to let her know he was

not about to go, "I made plans to go watch the game with my dad. You know the San Antonio Spurs play tonight."

Asia was pleased to hear that he already had plans. She looked him directly in his eyes, "I gotta call Shante. You know she don't like hanging out with Shannon and her wild ass friends. Plus, Shante be having problems when Shannon leaves Phat Daddy with his own daddy."

"That's crazy. How Shante mother doing?" Andre started some small talk.

"The same. She will probably never change. Shante just deal with her anyway."

Andre took a glance at his watch. The game was about to be on in an hour. He stood to let Asia know it was time for them to leave. He had to drop her off at home and there were at least twenty minutes from her house and his parents' house.

Asia pulled up in front of the Omni Majestic Hotel. The valet person ran over to her car. She exited her car and looked around, "A four star hotel. Um, I am impressed. He must be making a nice little stipend off those damn jokes."

Asia entered the lobby. She noticed the elevator doors were around the corner to her left. The establishment was extravagant. The aroma reminded her of a soft peppermint scent. She walked toward the elevator admiring how elegant everything was. The desk clerk nodded with a friendly smile. Asia returned the greeting with a smile as she pushed the up button on the elevator. Asia watched as she observed the floor the elevator was on before it got to her. The bell rang and the doors opened. Asia smiled as she entered the mirror surroundings.

Asia checked out her appearance. She was wearing the hell out of her gray wide leg wool Juicy Couture belted trousers. She adjusted her white with gray sequined cardigan. She unbuttoned the top button so she would be revealing a little cleavage. Right as the elevator doors opened, she realized that she had not even called to see if Omari was here or if he had changed his plans. She exited the elevator and looked at the room numbers. Where she would be going was to the left. She headed down the hall to room three one four. She slightly knocked on the door and there was no answer. She looked around noticing how empty the entire hallway was. Then she made another attempt to knock on the door. This time it was louder than the first. Still there was no answer. As she began to walk away thinking that Omari was about to miss out on something so special, the elevator dang and he made his exit. He was holding a small bag from Victoria Secret in one hand and a small CD player in the other hand.

Asia smiled as Omari approached her in his Borsalino Garibaldi newsboy patch cap. He was wearing an olive green suede jacket to match the olive green suede patch in newsboy cap. His dark rinsed relaxed fitted jeans were heavily starched. They look like they could stand-alone once he took them off. He was walking like Tyson Beckford on a New York runaway, as he got closer to her.

She could smell his alluring cologne. She bit her bottom lip, "Damn you smell good! What is that you are wearing?"

"It's a fragrance by Giorgio call Armani Code." Omari smiled knowing he smelled good. He opened the room door. Asia walked in as he held the door open. She continued to walk as he cut the lights on. She was beginning to think that Omari had a thing with the Victorian era. His mother's home had Victorian furniture and now he had brought her to a room that was filled with Victorian furniture. She wasn't surprised by his taste once she found out he was a fan of Prince. He was far different from the previous people that she encountered.

He plugged up the radio near the bed and pulled out

the bra and panty set from the bag. The sounds of Prince's *Controversy* album softly escaped from the speakers. He looked at Asia as she took a seat on the Queen Size bed. He smirked, "Go shower." He reached in the bag, pulled out a bottle of Blossoming Romance, and tossed it on the bed.

Asia was not in the shower long. She completely dried off before she put on the lingerie. She came out the bathroom wearing a purple lace thong, the matching purple lace bra, and her black closed toe Gianna Meliani high heels. She moved her body to Prince's rhythm as he sang *Do Me, Baby.*

Omari readjusted himself in his black boxer briefs. He watched as Asia gyrated to the soothing sounds of his favorite artists. She was working it for him. There was only one thing missing, the pole. He slowly licked his top lip, "I did very well. I really didn't know what size to get. I had one of those scenes going when Will Smith was in Enemy of the State picking out something for his wife. I told this female that you were about her size and I see I was very correct. Come over here so I can rub this lotion on you."

Asia laid down on her back as he began to massage the lotion on every part of her body. The tenderness of his hands turned her on immediately. As he continued to rub her inner thigh, she began to tingle. She thought to herself, "This was not right." Andre was watching the game and she was about to get her freak on with someone else. He slid his tongue around the inner side of her thigh and she made up in her mind that she was not going home that night.

She wasn't very happy when she heard about Omari's relocation plans. Nevertheless, she was relieved on the account of Andre, to hear that Omari was leaving for LA in the next two weeks. Within those two weeks, they quickly became cutty buddies. He was kidnapping that kitty katt and she came up with an extremely good alibi every time Andre would question her whereabouts. She made sure she called him when she wanted that good shit. Although he didn't take her to H-town like T-Pain sang, but he made her coochie feel like la la la. He had to pursue his career and it was not going to happen for him in his hometown. After that love making session, Andre was going to be in a little trouble. He had some competition on his hands and he didn't even know about it. Omari had definitely popped Asia's juice box.

Shante looked at Asia as she smiled about her thoughts. "Asia, did that boy have five inches for real?"

"Hell naw. He had every bit of twelve. I wanted to tell his ass give me six now and I'll be back tomorrow for the other six." Asia laughed so hard. Shante couldn't help but laugh right along with her. Asia couldn't believe that she had forgotten about him. He should have been on the top of her list. Had she been listing the names in the order of best to worst, he would have been number one, but she wasn't going in that order.

"Girl you need to call your mother and see what she wants before she put an APB out on you." Asia stops laughing as she thought about Shante's mother.

"She doesn't want anything but some damn Crown. She needs an all points bulletin stating there has been a prohibition on alcohol."

Asia looked over at Shante. Asia was trying to hold back her laughter. Shante's mother did drink a tad bit too much. Asia could not recall one time that she had ever seen her sober. She figured that was one reason Shante never really drank anything.

Asia looked out the window and up to the sky. She noticed the one shining star that appeared to be blinking. She wondered what was her Aunt Wanda doing and had she found happiness. She figured she must have because she never heard a thing from her since she left her Uncle Rob. Then her thoughts left Wanda and she began to think about her very own mother. She gazed at the star and she wished she could just talk to her and see if she was okay. Most of her life she resented her mother for leaving her. She tried so hard not to even think about her and so far, it worked.

Asia could hear her mother telling her to look to the stars whenever she got lonely and she would be there to comfort her. She never felt the comfort the first few times she looked at the stars, so she never looked again, until now. She didn't know what made her look up and notice this star, but she wished she could snatch it out the air and make it stop blinking.

Asia glared over in Shante's direction, "Do you want to know what my mother told me on the day she left me?"

Shante took a glimpse at Asia. She didn't want to look in her eyes because she wasn't ready for the crying fest that she believed that would soon follow. Shante let out a sigh, "Asia, what did she say to you?"

Asia chuckled with hurt, "She told me to look to the stars whenever I get lonely. What the fuck was the star suppose to tell me. Was that damn star going to tell me that the spot in my panties was my menstrual cycle? That damn star couldn't take me to the got damn store and buy me some kotex. That star couldn't teach me right from wrong. Not one time, did I ever hear that star tell me, it loved me. You know when I look to the stars; all I could see was a star that was happy. It was like that mother fucking star was saying na nanny na na I am so fucking happy."

Shante took a deep breath. She held her lips tightly together. She was holding in her tears. She wanted to cry, but Asia broke out with a loud burst of laughter. She was truly laughing to keep from crying. It had been a long time since they had one of these sentimental moments. Shante thought they had left that back in their adolescence stage. She realized that her mother wasn't going to ever change and she took her for what she was worth. Asia knew nothing of her mother. She didn't know if she likes to drink or if she hated the smell of alcohol. She didn't know what not to do to make her mother curse her out. Shante thought about not knowing her father. Asia didn't know either one of her parents. It was as though she needed to see her mother for a brief period of her life and that was it.

Chapter 21

PAUL

Another day of surveillance was back on. Shante and Asia pulled on the parking lot of the Royal Palace. Shante was trying to figure out why she had never acted upon her thoughts about coming to the spot that he loved to hang out. Willie tried to portray the image of a corporate man who didn't tolerate those he presumed wasn't of his caliber. He found himself flossing in his Escalade and his Red Monkey attire. He was very proud of working hard to afford the finest of the finer things he wanted. Only his appearance fit the description of corporate man during the day and thug at night. His attitude and presence only complemented the status Shante maintained.

Even though he wasn't on time for anything, leaving in advance was one thing he would certainly do. Just as Shante thought, he exited the club before the last call of alcohol. Had he known what type of night he was in for he would have answered that last call and took that last drink. The girls exited the car with Louisville slugger and department issue Berretta in tow.

Before he could react, he was brought to his knees from the slug. He began to try to crawl for his life but the hands that were now pulling him in the opposite direction had him confused. He was ordered to get in the trunk of the car. Being at gunpoint, he did what was being instructed of him. He simply obliged.

As Asia slammed the trunk, she and Shante became startled by someone screaming.

"Asia!" the person exiting the club screamed.

Asia turned around to see who was screaming her name. She smiled when she saw that it was her longtime friend, Paul.

"What's up with you Paul?" Asia walked toward him looking back at Shante like everything was cool.

Shante was watching nervously. She watched Asia like a dope fiend trying to comp a high and didn't come with all the money. She was standing by the car thinking, "We do not have time for her to be conversing with anyone." Shante was growing impatient. She watched as Asia and this fellow were in deep conversation. They seem to be having the time of their life. When she hugged him and said her good-byes, Shante frantically awaited her arrival at the car.

"Calm down Brown Suga." Asia smiled as she got in the car.

The sounds of screeching tires on pavement were all that was heard. Five miles down the road sirens flared. Shante pulled over as they waited on the officer to make his next move sounds of beating in the trunk escaped through the car.

Shante looked over at Asia wondering what to do next. Asia took a deep breath and exited the car.

The officer watched as she approached him. Asia had remembered the officer's face, but couldn't remember what precinct he was from. Asia looked directly at his badge.

"Good evening Officer Dixon. Can you tell me why you are pulling me and my friend over?" Asia stood waiting on his response.

"Hello, the future Mrs. Townsend." he couldn't think of her name, he just knew she was a dispatcher at the main precinct and she was usually the one who handled the records check. He did know that she was engaged to a coworker of his. He was bad at names anyway and Asia knew it. "Well, I stopped you guys because you were driving extremely fast and swerving at the same time. You ladies had too much to drink, I see."

Asia smiled, "Just celebrating my big day to come."

"I see. Congratulations and drive carefully."

Asia walked back to the car and waved as he drove off.

"Pop the trunk." Asia instructed Shante.

Asia silenced the noise. When Asia sat back down in the car, she gave Shante a look that let her know everything was okay. Shante pulled off into the traffic.

"Oh, Paul." Asia leaned back with a smile on her face. Asia decided to retire from her game since Andre was home. Andre and his folks got her hooked up as a dispatcher when he made it home. It was her first day on the job; she bumped into Paul looking for directions to make his friend's bond. He entered the building all in such a frantic frenzy. His fast paced, walk and loud fretting voice caught her attention.

Asia stopped him in his tracks. He was amazed with her attractiveness. Along with her giving him instructions on where he needed to be, and he got her phone number. He was looking like Asia's favorite celebrity.

This was the first time Asia would have to figure out how she was going to engage in some new sexual recreation. Andre was always away at school when she was doing her thing. With him being away, that alone didn't fall in her category of cheating. She considered him being away meant that they could see other people. He never said that but that was what she told herself. Now, in the past, she found the excuse of helping Andre out in school and that's why she did what she did. She was proud when he graduated knowing that she contributed in part to his professional growth.

She didn't need to go see Paul because Andre satisfied every need. She just wanted to know if she had lost her touch.

After a few telephone conversations, they eventually made a date. Agreeing that they would meet at his place because she didn't want to be seen in any public place, she arrived promptly at six. She was cool because Andre was working from three to eleven. He didn't call as much during his shift.

Asia walked up to the door. When he said he could cook she didn't believe it. The aroma of something appetizing greeted her at the door. She walked in because he had already informed her that the door would be open and she just needed to come in.

The arrangement of his house was nice. All the rooms were painted in a bold color of either sage green or money green. All the borders were accented with a bright cream paint with a Victorian design. Each piece of furniture coincided with one another. The furniture was Victorian.

One thing had put Asia on the edge. It was the picture of a woman that looked to be younger than Paul was. There was some sort of resemblances between the both of them. Same caramel complexion and heart shape lips. Her eyes seemed to be wide open and not slanted. She thought about the female just being his sister, but she was definitely going to ask. Thoughts of her last encounter with someone's significant other surfaced. Asia remembered telling herself that she would never put herself in that type of situation again.

She maneuvered her way to the kitchen area. There she found her Jamie Foxx look-a-like grilling in the Kitchen area. Asia thought about Shante telling her how she could never understand why somebody that made an ugly woman turned her friend on. They laughed all the time at the fact that Asia's

Aunt Wanda shared the same name as the character Jamie Foxx played on *In Living Color*.

Asia was stunned that Andre's name was coming across the screen. She stared hard at the screen wishing the phone would stop ringing. She wondered if he could feel that she was doing something wrong, now that he wasn't several miles away.

Paul noticed the hesitant look that grew upon her face. "You are not going to answer? That's the number one rule. Never ignore a call."

It stopped ringing. Asia kept her eyes on the phone anticipating the next ring. This time she would be prepared to answer. Once it rang, she was ready for whatever Andre was about to say or ask.

"Hello." Asia looked at Paul wishing he remained quiet. The devilish look she was giving him, he knew not to say a word anyway.

"I was just calling to let you know to meet me at my house tonight. I have a surprise for you." Andre spoke with enthusiasm.

"Okay. Is eleven thirty fine?" Asia didn't want to remain on the phone long. She was going to keep this call short and sweet.

"That's cool. See you then. Love you."

"Love you, too." Asia hung up the phone.

"Whatcha over here burning?" Asia moved in to see what he was doing over the range.

"Burning? Girl, you looking at the Chef Boyar Paul!" Paul smiled.

"What you about to feed me?" Asia didn't care if it was good or not. She was ready to eat because everything smelled good.

"We are having Caribbean Spiced Ribs along with Spicy Noodles and Cabbage Stir-Fry in an oyster sauce. For dessert," he walked over to the counter top and grabbed a cake pan, "my favorite German Chocolate Cake." He smiled admiring his accomplishments of a well-cooked meal.

Asia didn't turn down food. Now she was thinking about the photographs and was wondering if her nice dinner would be interrupted.

"Who's the girl in the pictures?" Asia studied Paul's facial expression.

"Latina."

Asia waited to see if he was going to follow up with an explanation. He continued to prepare their dinner. He walked pass Asia to the dinner area and placed the condiments on the table.

Asia leaned up against the wall and you could see the heart formation of her lips. She folded her arms and contemplated on leaving, but she needed an answer. She was not about to play this game. She could go to Andre's parents' house and wait on him while visiting with his mother. She had been in remission for a few years now, and Asia like hearing how good she was doing. They could catch up on some needed conversation.

Just as she was headed to the door, he spoke, "She's not coming home anytime soon. She's tied up at the moment."

That's when he went into detail about why he was at the police station. Latina had been caught hustling on the block. Paul had found him a straight hood chic. She was on the block and was about to be charged with intent to distribute crack-cocaine. This was her third time being caught and things weren't working out in her favor. Asia couldn't say anything because she found herself being similar to Latina under a different circumstance.

Paul told her how much he was against her hustling, but his love for her wouldn't allow him to leave her. They had a bond every since the age of five. That's when Asia was trying to figure out why Paul had Asia in their home. When she asked, he let her know it wasn't about sex. He just wanted to talk because Asia reminded him of Latina. Latina never would listen to what he had to say. Asia was looking at him like, "Why should she listen."

Asia just knew she had lost it. All Paul wanted was a conversation.

He sat across the dining room table watching Asia eat. She was enjoying every bit of it. When Asia was about to take a sip of the Rothschild Pauillac Wine, Paul was ready to talk.

"This is good." Asia was amazed by the taste of the wine.

He smiled, "You know that Jesus turned water into wine to prove that He's the source of life. As he changed the water to wine, He offered a symbol of the new spiritual life that Jesus brings from the old mortal in conversion. This is where many people make a mistake. They want to improve themselves in to being worthy of everything else before they accept Christ. In reality, it's in accepting Jesus as the Savior that God counts us worthy of entering his presence."

Asia looked and she wanted to hear more. She had gone to church a couple of times and believed that there was a high power, but she had never gotten into the word until today. Paul was intriguing her intellectually.

Paul continued to talk, "Last Sunday, I went to church and the Pastor's sermon came from John 3:16, For God so loved the world, that he gave his only begotten Son, that whosoever believeth in him should not perish, but have everlasting life." He paused for a minute making sure he had Asia's attention. Then he continued, "You know this is one of the most widely quoted verses from the Bible. It has been called the Gospel in a nutshell. If you don't remember anything else always remember, first and foremost, God loves you and you are His little precious creation. He doesn't care what is in the past that you may have done. It is time for the past to remain in the past move on with Him because He has a plan for us all!"

Asia took a deep breath. She knew exactly why she was here and it wasn't by choice. Wherever he was going with his conversation, she needed to hear it.

He went on, "You don't need a man to define who you are. No one completes you, but you. Now, a man may compliment you, but he never completes you. You have lost yourself, but now it's time to find Asia and love her. Once you can forgive yourself, anything else shouldn't matter."

He took a sip of his wine. Asia was focused on every word that left his mouth. He looked directly into her eyes, "I can tell that things aren't easy for you right now. You may be wondering how you are going to deal with everything that you are facing, but I know you have a strong spirit and even though it may seem as though it is hard for you to understand, I know you have exactly what it takes to get through it. I know I am probably skipping around a little, but follow me." Paul looked at Asia to make sure she was following along.

Paul continued to talk, "The Pastor went along with her sermon talking about knowing GOD. He said as a young boy, he had a lot of questions, "Wanting to know why." As he became older, he developed an understanding. He said he has been walking along a path for a while during his journey. Along that path, he walked with foolishness, pleasure, faith, and forgiveness. Faith and forgiveness helped him to understand his foolish pleasures. All things work together for good and if it's truly for us, nothing will stand in the way of it."

Asia began to think about her past. She realized that in the beginning, she had no reasons for her actions, but it eventually became a cause. Asia personally benefited from it but it wasn't just for her. It was for the one she so deeply loved. She prayed that Andre never found out about the acts she committed, but if he did, she would have to come clean.

Paul was bringing his little sermon to an end, "There are many men out there leaving their daughters without a father figure. Some girls make it through and others fall weak. They go searching to fill the void and these boys that don't know anything about being a man, use them. Always remember, boys do what they can and men do what they want. You should only settle for someone that appreciates you, for you and respects you for who you are. Now, I can go on and on and talk about how worthless some men are, but I will save that for another day. While on your journey and as you grow closer to GOD, you will gain more of an understanding."

For the remainder of the night, they sat and talked. Asia even mentioned her desire of becoming a fashion designer. Paul let her know that dreams can come true, but if you never do anything about it how will you ever know. He simply was encouraging her to let the whole fashion idea leave the thought process stage. When Asia left, he told her, that if she ever need to talk again or needed the support of a friend he would be there with his listening ears, a shoulder to lean on and open arms. From that day on, conversation and friendship was all that went on between them. She could not believe she found a male friend and all they did was talk. She almost talked past the time she had set to leave so that she could meet Andre.

They pulled up at the same time. She planned on going in talking to his mother but it was now too late. The dinner had her tired. Andre didn't want anything but to drive around and look at houses and he thought he had found the perfect house.

##########

Asia was happy to hear that Latina had gotten herself together and they were about to have their second child. That's when she knew that she needed to talk to Andre. All the conversations that she and Paul ever had came to mind. She was going to his house and she was not taking no for an answer.

"Shante take me to Andre's house!"

"Do you realize that Willie's in the trunk?" Shante had a look of bewilderment.

"He isn't dead. He has been hit with a bat a couple of times. He alright." Asia waved her hand, "I could have shot his ass and ended all that misery."

"He could have died from shock." Shante showed a sign of concern.

"You could have died from shock, but your ass still breathing. This nigga has lied to you for the last couple of years. He basically sold you a dream. He playing house with his real family and you out her catering to this sorry ass nigga's every need. Then you see his punk ass and he can't even be a man in the whole situation. You wanna go hard and wait on the nigga coming out the club. Besides, who else can help us with this, other than the police?" Asia looked at Shante, thinking about what she was about to tell her ex-finance.

Shante did as instructed and headed toward Andre's house. The black version of Thelma and Louise was about to pop off. Shante knew it was no turning back now.

Shante pulled up in front of Andre's house. Shante waited on Asia's next move, it never came. Shante drove to the nearest gas station. After filling up, Asia told her to pull over in a dark area. Shante pulled right under a tree behind the rest area of the gas station.

"Pop the trunk!" Asia got out as Shante hit the switch to open the trunk. She felt around his neck to check for a pulse. She was so relieved when she felt that he still had a pulse and it was beating at a steady pace. Willie was sound asleep.

Shante decided to get a room. She pulled the car right

outside the window of room 106. Asia walked in and laid across the bed. She was killing her brain cells with all the thinking she was doing. Not one day in her life had she ever had to think this hard.

"We need to tie him up. If he comes to, he can kick his way out of the car."

Shante kept a straight razor to make sure her eyebrows were always on point. She started cutting up the towels and the sheets in the hotel room. They pulled around the corner. Asia jabbed him in the gut with the bat one good time. His body jerked but he didn't open his eyes.

Back at the hotel, Asia thought she could get some rest and think about their next move now that Willie was all tied up. She thought about the weather. It wasn't as cold as it had been. The weather was changing but it was still a little nippy. She told Shante to take him a blanket out there. It was two o'clock a.m. and they would be leaving by five a.m. anyway. Shante found some humor in Asia saying the cold weather wouldn't hurt a dog for three hours.

Chapter 22

NEWS YOU CAN USE

"Good Morning, if you have just tuned in here's what you have missed." The news broadcaster switched to a news newscaster who was standing in front of the St. Louis Metropolitan Police Department.

"Innocent or guilty is what they are inside trying to determine. Chief Ruble Steele ends a 24-year career with the St. Louis Police Department. He started as a rookie on the streets in September 1979 and rose through the ranks to Chief of Police on December 11, 2003. Now he's retiring. Why? This could be answered with several answers. There are several speculations. He and several unknown police officers are the center focus of a federal investigation."

Asia rose from the bed. She thought she was dreaming until she saw the expression on Shante's face.

"You think Andre apart of that mess?" Shante waited on Asia's response.

"I seriously doubt that. Andre doesn't have a wrong bone in his body. Not saying he can't do any wrong. But he is not about to break any regulations." Asia was defending Andre.

"So how are we going to take a kidnapped man to him so he help us?" Shante was confused.

Asia wasn't worried. Andre wasn't any boy scout but he did play by the rules.

Andre was throwing several glasses of Crown down his throat. He was worried that he might be guilty by association. He told Aaron, Darryl, and Darrell that they need to leave the Chief's son alone.

He tried to tell them that taking cars from the police impound custody and selling them below market value was a big mistake and was going to eventually have them under a criminal investigation. The Chief's son had a hook up with a towing company that handled the impounded cars. They would pull cats over flossing in their shoes. Nine times out of ten, things weren't right with the car. The tow trucks would pick up the vehicle and ship them to Kansas City to get a makeover and back to the Lou, to resale. These cats found themselves buying cars they probably owned at one time or either or one of their partners's owned it.

Andre needed to talk to Asia. She was the only one he could confess to and didn't have to worry about someone finding out. He reminisced on how he would lay down and tell no one but Asia his true feelings.

Andre had tossed and turned the entire night. He was missing holding Asia close to him. He wanted her more and more. He could feel her touch. She loved him straight from her heart and he knew it. He needed to talk to her more than ever. It was time to reconcile.

Andre knew that all his secrets were safe with her. He hoped that the connection was still there. She couldn't throw it all away in this short length time. He thought about how he was going to speak to her and if she would listen. She was definitely the pages of his diary. He wasn't worried about the investigation because he had nothing to do with the crime. He just needed to talk. His worries were based on whether or not that Asia would want to talk to him. She was undeniably his security.

"What's on the agenda?" Shante desperately wanted to know what they were going to do next. Shante was thinking that they should just kill him and dump his body somewhere. Whatever Asia had in store, she knew that Asia would see to it that it be completed. Ever since they were kids, they have honored each other by their loyalty toward one another.

As they were about to exit the hotel room, William Crawford's picture flashed a crossed the screen. They both looked at each other in nervousness. Shante didn't expect it to go this far and neither did Asia. Someone had reported him missing. Why the urgency, they both thought? He hadn't been missing for the full twenty-four hours.

Shante became furious. She knew that it had to be the other woman that Willie had fathered his children with. She wanted this to be over and it had to end soon. People would start calling her about his disappearance. The last person Shante wanted to inquiry about Willie was Andre or any of his relatives. Just on the strength of the relationship that Shante had with the family, an Amber alert would go in affect for a grown washed up man. The last thing she needed was for the entire police department to be in search of him.

Chapter 23

YOU GOT ME WIDE OPEN

Andre lie awake in his bed staring at the ceiling. He thought about Regina and the child at the crime scene. Under the circumstances, he never had the opportunity to even mention Regina to Asia. He didn't even know if he ever wanted to tell her. Regardless to what Asia did, he cheated and a baby could have been conceived. Experiencing the situation and seeing the resemblance of a familiar face had him thinking all kinds of things. He had produced a baby that he never had the opportunity to meet. Could he even share that with his mother? Although she was sick, she was still fighting for her life and to be told that she was possibly the grandmother of a homicide victim wouldn't be in her best interest.

He thought about his relationship with Asia. The list was not really worth throwing everything they had away. The ring of the doorbell nearly startled him. He laid there until it rang again. He envisioned that he was being swarmed by SWAT. The third time it rang he gathered himself up to answer. He figured that if it were the police they would be in by now.

Through the bay window, he could see Shante's car. He didn't expect to see Asia as he eased the door open. When he looked toward the car that's when he noticed Shante still sitting in the car.

"How are you?" Asia waited patiently for his response.

Everything in her just wanted to run to him, wrap her arms around him, and tell him she missed him and how much she loved him.

Right when Andre was about to speak, Asia produced the little notebook. She pushed it up to his chest. "I want you to read every one of those names and remember them. They all got you through college. All them money wires and transfers. The trips to get you back home. The extra care baskets that's where it came from. You know I thought about this all night. I didn't know what I was going to say to you until now. I have one question. Tell me this. Why you never ask me where I was getting all the money from? Not one time did you even ask me. You were fine with the fact you were being taking care of, but now you want to look down on me." tears started to form.

Andre took the notebook and walked to the kitchen. Asia could smell the fire. She walked in and saw him standing over the stove with her little red notebook in flames. She was right, he never asked where the money came from and at this point he didn't care.

Andre embraced Asia tightly. He sealed the statement with a long awaited kiss. He knew if Asia would have found out what had taken place during his college years, she would have forgiven him. Asia truly loved him unconditionally and he knew it.

Shante sat in the car becoming paranoid. She watched the door seeing if Asia was about to return. Ten minutes had passed, but she had the feeling as if she had been waiting for at least thirty minutes. She was experiencing a feeling that she hadn't felt in a long time. The feeling of disgust invaded her. It was the same feeling that she underwent when Keith and Tyrone tormented her years ago.

Never in a million years would anyone tell her that Willie would have her feeling this way. She was fumbling with her thoughts to see if there had been any signs of deceit.

Nothing emerged. She was ready to rid herself from all the hurt. She didn't need any remembrance of Willie. She was ready to execute on her thoughts.

Now twenty minutes had gone by and still no Asia. She pondered on her next move. Departing from her car, she could hear the sounds of sirens. Walking to the back of the car, she raised the trunk. Willie eyes were wide open. The small sheet prevented him from talking. He pleaded for his life with sincerity in his eyes.

She looked directly at him. Ready to make an emphasizing effort on every letter of the words she was about to speak, "Mother fucker you gone to regret that you ever met Shante Irby." She slammed the trunk of her car. She was ready to take matters in her own hands. She was hurting and whatever Asia had planned wouldn't resolve her issue. She needed to do it all on her own.

Shante entered Andre's house. She could hear sounds coming from the kitchen area. She came in and interrupted it all.

"MMM MMM. Did you forget something?" Shante stood with her hand on her hip.

Asia grinned, "Andre, I have to show you something."

The sounds of the sirens brought them all to the front door. Shante grabbed Asia's hand to prevent her from going outside. Asia nodded her head telling her that everything was fine. All of a sudden, Shante thought about the surveillance camera that the Royal Palace had. The three of them exited the house together. There were several police cars in front of the residence. They found themselves swarmed by the men in blue.

Chapter 24

NEVER KNEW IT COULD BE DAYS LIKE THIS

Shante sat in her car. She was piping hot. The car was running but there was no heat coming through the vents. Asia made a lot of sense but that was not what she wanted to hear. She was now wondering what her and Andre was discussing when she left her outside for so long. Asia told her to hold tight till after the cops left. They were going to find some place to put the car and douse it with gasoline. Willie was going to be burned alive. His washed up ass would never hurt anyone again.

Together they sat and listen to the police stories. The officers that were on duty came to see if their colleague was okay after hearing all disturbing news about the Chief of Police. No one in their circle would be implicated in their involvement. The chief was just going to step down.

Shante didn't care about the conversation that was taking place. She sat looking out the window of her car becoming bent out of shape. There were over ten police officers standing approximately twenty feet from a kidnapped victim being held against his will in the trunk of a car.

All the time they rode to an unknown destination, Shante was wondering how committed Asia would be in assisting her with her problem. In seconds she grew furious thinking that Asia was about to attempt her first act of betrayal with her.

Shante pulled up on the Royal Palace parking lot. She looked at Asia and her face became flushed. She didn't move. There was still an opportunity to burn the car with Willie in it.

"Shante, what are you waiting on?" Asia looked at her friend.

"Asia, you cannot be serious. He still can call the police." Shante searched for some understanding.

"We were just in a house with the law. You just heard about all that crookedness. No one is going to be implicated in anything. This way it will work in our favor. Now you either going to pop the trunk and let him go or I'll do it for you!"

"Asia let me know what changed your mine. We were just standing talking about how we were going to end this. You came up with burning the car. You came up with that. Not me! You!"

"Shante, all I can say is that, "Last night I asked for forgiveness. With that, I promised no more transgression. It was no coincidence that I bumped into Paul last night. That was simply a revelation." Asia gathered her thoughts. She was about to lie to her friend for the very first time in life. Paul said some things to her that made her realize she needed to start going in a new direction and she was ready to admit that she needed some new direction. She knew Shante was not ready to hear her take on life right now. She wanted results and she needed them fast. Asia knew her friend was hurting and she was about to act upon her hurt and leave a lot more others hurting.

She looked Shante directly in her eyes, "You want more certainty and closure in your life right now, but it's hard. Willie didn't play by the rules and it didn't seem to meet your expectations. You are about to play a game of baseball with your life, but only in this game, it will be one strike and you are out. Ultimately all this tension will pass. I know it is difficult for you to concentrate because your mind is bouncing around all over the place. You know what Paul told me," Asia didn't give her time to respond, "You make a wish and work really hard to make it come true."

"I wish his ass was dead!" Shante screamed.

That was not the answer she was looking for. She had chosen the wrong words. Asia snatched the keys from the ignition and walked to the back of the car. She opened the trunk of the car and Willie looked terrified. She informed him that she was going to untie him and he could go. Asia looked around to see if anyone was looking. Willie's Escalade was parked next to a dark green two door Tahoe. Asia walked to the front of the car. She noticed Shante brown skin was drenched with tears.

"Shante, how long has that truck been sitting on this parking lot?"

"I think it pulled up when you opened the trunk."

Shante moved from the side of the car. She walked to the back of the car and noticed that Willie couldn't move. Asia decided to phone Andre.

Asia let Andre know that she needed him right away. He let her know he would get there as soon as possible. On his drive up to the Royal Palace, he had a funny feeling.

Shante pulled her car around so that she would be facing the Tahoe. No movement could be seen coming from the truck. Andre pulled on the lot at high-speed. Asia and Shante got out the car and stood by the trunk of the car.

Andre placed his hands in his black jogging pants and walked around to the back of the car with the girls. He looked at them following their eyes to Willie's body.

"What the hell is he doing in your trunk?" Andre looked at Shante. He turned to look down at Willie, "Dude, you okay?" He reached in to grab his hands. He was so cramped in the trunk of the car he could barely move. Andre struggled getting him out and proceeded to walk him to his truck. The passenger door of the truck opened as Andre walked back toward the girls.

Shante saw the same short female with the protruding hips that was at the clinic with Willie and the kids. Things moved so fast. The female walked swiftly up to Willie's driver door. She opened the door and shots rang out. Soon after she fired the gun, she yelled, "Yo black ass will never cheat on me again!"

The Tahoe speed off the lot at stop speed before the girl even closed the door. Asia stood in amazement and Andre called for reinforcement. Shante ran over to Willie's truck screaming and hollering. She tried to hold him up as he was about to slump his body over the steering wheel.

"Willie, hang in there! I can't do this without you! Baby I am so sorry! I never meant to hurt you! I just wanted you to feel what I was feeling! Pleeeeassse baby hang in there!" Shante screamed as she held on to Willie. She was becoming soaked with his blood. His eyes rolled to the back of his head and he looked at Shante with a dead stare. She took a deep breath and closed his eyelids.

When the paramedics reached the scene and took his pulse. They immediately began the resuscitation process. Willie did not respond. That's when they realized there was nothing left for them to do. Shante stood by his side to the very end. She was having some very erratic thoughts about the entire night. She wanted to hurt him but this was not what she had in plan. Honestly, she didn't know what was going to happen to him if they had continued their night. Shante was so glad that Willie didn't die by her hands or the hands that belonged to Asia. She released him and walked toward Asia. Asia embraced her as her tears began to roll down her face.

Willie died at the scene. She shot him six times. The first bullet did the most damage when it struck him in his heart. The others just rippled through hitting him near his lungs and kidneys. Homicide arrived at the scene along with the crime unit. Andre didn't want to be questioned at the moment so he informed Asia that he was ready to go.

"Shante, I don't know what to say to you right now," Asia looked at her friend not holding back a single tear, "we are getting ready to leave and we won't you to come with us."

Shante watched as Asia and Andre drove off. She denied their request in taking her home. She wanted to be alone. She needed to regroup and think her life through. She had walked side by side with foolishness for quite some time and now she was about to walk side by side with forgiveness. She just needed the strength to move forward. She realized that letting Asia and Andre leave and releasing Willie from the trunk of her car was not a good idea. Every officer that came and asked a question she let them know what had happened, as she closed with, "Everything thing just moved so fast. He wouldn't have been able to respond because she approached him at a very high speed. I don't even think he saw her coming." Shante stayed at the scene until the last officer left. He let her know that they would be contacting her very soon.

She got in her car and drove to Andre's house. She was glad to see that they had made it. When she knocked on the door Andre's brother, Aaron, answered. He embraced her tightly. A feeling of warmth fulfilled her soul. Today she had finally found the feeling of peace.

She looked in to Aaron's eyes, "I never knew it could be days like this."

Aaron held her tightly, "You are going to get to know a lot more days like this one!"

He felt bad for her but he was able to approach her. That was something he wanted to do a long time ago. He was aware of their friendship and he didn't want to jeopardize their friendship. He always told himself he would wait on his moment and it had finally come.

~ 206 ~

Chapter 25

SOMEDAY

Shante stood looking in the mirror. This is the first time in a long while that she had looked in the mirror and was happy with what she saw. A day that she knew would come had eventually come. She would be putting her mother to rest. Her mother had cirrhosis of the liver. After more than a decade of heavy drinking, her liver began to function improperly and other organs began to fail. When Shannon phoned her to let her know that she had found their mother sitting slumped in the recliner, Shante was at peace. Her mother had her experiencing irritation, disharmony, and agitation. This was certainly an improper way to live. She learned to deal with it and Asia helped her cope with it.

Throughout her life, unwanted things tend to have happened to her. Not once did she ever try to understand why things always seemed to happen to her. She didn't like the cards that life had dealt. She never dwelled on the fact of the torture that Asia's cousins put here through. She completely forgot about the laughing they were doing with all of their ranting. She simply closed her eyes and prayed that it had quickly come to an end. Throughout her life, she simply shut her eyes to many things, but when Willie deceived her, she was no longer going to sleep on anything else. Shante felt fortunate to have Asia in her life. At some points in her life, she thought her fate was only determined by Asia because she had always been there for her. The atmosphere she was surrounding herself with, eventually became permeated with peace and harmony.

She could see Aaron lying in bed sound asleep. She gave him a smile. He had envied his brother's relationship for a long time, but now he had found love. The love that he found was going to do nothing but love him. Shante no longer felt that she needed Asia's protection or her pity. For some strange reason, she was able to detach from all the negative situations. She prayed that she would remain peaceful and happy. What she was now praying for, she had previously wished for before, Willie was let out of the trunk of her car.

Just for a second, she thought about Willie. She hated that his wife was about to face trial for his murder. Things didn't look so good for her. Shante's heart went out to her because the love that she had for him was about to put herself in that exact same situation. Life had dealt her a bad hand. She had practically called misdeal a long time ago, but tried so desperately to turn it into a good hand. All attempts failed. Asia had come through like always because had she not decided to let him go, Shante knew the cards were stacked against him. Shante stood looking in the mirror wearing a great big kool-aid smile. Aaron had talked about children the night before. This was something she had never given a thought. She tried to talk her sister out of having her child, but Shannon didn't listen. Shante supported her the best way she could.

"Why are you just standing there?" Aaron asked while lying in bed. He had opened his eyes and noticed that she was just stuck admiring herself. In all the years of them knowing one another, he had never gained the courage to step to her. When they sat and talked about Asia and Andre at Culpeppers he looked into her eyes and knew right then, choosing her would be the right choice. He was reacting upon his gut feeling. Looking at how peacefully Shante was, he knew going with his gut feeling was the best way to go.

Chapter 26

TYING UP ALL LOSE ENDS

Janice stood looking out of her apartment window. Her heart shape lips were pierced together. She had read the headline TWENTY-FOUR YEAR OLD MURDER UNCOVERED, repeatedly. Would it be the answer that she longed for? As she stood looking out of the window, she found the North Star shining brighter than it ever had. She picked back up the newspaper and looked to the star, "Anthony, is this your story? Will my questions be answered? Will you ever forgive me for deserting our child?"

Asia lay comfortably in the warmth of Andre's arms. There was no other place that she would have rather been. She was so glad that Shante understood her opposing the death of Willie. Asia couldn't explain what had come over her and made her change her mind about the annihilation of Willie. The flashing of a light caught Asia's attention. She rose from the bed and walked over to the window. Asia stood looking out of Andre's bedroom window as she noticed the star shining ever so bright.

"When I was a little girl, my mother use to tell me whenever I saw a star shining so bright, to make a wish, for that star was going to see that I would never be lonely?" Asia closed her eyes.

Andre walked over to the window to join her. He wrapped his arms around her as he stood behind, "What you wish for?"

"If I tell you my wish won't come true!" Asia laughed.

"Well I hope that this trial goes well for the Chief."

"Why wouldn't it?" Asia didn't understand why he would be thinking things would not work in his favor.

"They are bringing all kinds of things up. They are even bringing up a murder that took place over twenty-four years ago. They are talking about many forced retirements of anyone that can be implemented or tied to him. That's not good for my dad or my uncles. They all use to be partners back in the day." Andre walked over to the bed and sat down. To him, a name meant everything and this would be another issued he felt that he would be dealing with. He didn't want his family to be embarrassed by him. If they were implicated in any of the chief's crimes, he didn't know if father could take it.

Asia didn't know how to console him. In all reality, she wanted to tell him that wasn't his problem, but she didn't want to throw salt on an open wound. Andre hadn't asked Asia any questions about the list in her notebook. She knew he was trying to put all that behind the two of them. She didn't want to have the feeling of walking on eggshells if she told him that he was worrying about the wrong and most irrelevant things.

Robert was preparing for his day in court. He had been subpoenaed to court on an issue he thought would never be uncovered. He could remember the day when he had to tell his sister that her child's father had been murdered. He felt as though all this was his fault. This was one of the reasons that he never turned Asia away and he never went looking for Janice.

He was setting up a deal that he thought would have him set for the rest of his life. He was trying to make the only man he knew as his father rich. His foster family did many illegal things as far as gambling and boosting anything that they could sale at a discounted price. He was about to introduce them to the dope game. The only problem was that the seller was the St. Louis Metropolitan Police. While about to make their exchange, the radio that one rookie was carrying was not turned off. Before the money was about to be exchanged a robbery in progress was being announced. Seconds later, the robber entered into gun battle that everyone escaped but Anthony. He was pronounced dead on the scene, shot by the rookie that eventually became the Chief of Police.

From that day forward, Robert couldn't do anything right. His foster family went as far as disowning him, but they never put him out on the street. The only work he was allowed to do was minor. He worked at the family's body shop fixing flats on cars. This day would be the day he could finally complete a task and didn't have to worry about messing it up.

NO YOUR STATUS. GET TESTED.

The commercial played over and over in Asia's head as Andre drove the car to the courthouse. He was running late. He had over slept. He forgot to tell Asia that he was planning on going to the Chief's hearing. The original plan was to go to the health department so they could be tested. Asia let him know that she wanted to come along anyway. This was something that she didn't want to put on the back burner. The health department was on the way to the court building. She let him know that she was going to court with him. She was going to support him. She wanted to be there for him if he heard any disturbing news. Asia didn't know what all had taken place with Andre and the police department, but she figured something was going on because Andre was making it his business to be there. If she would have asked him, he would have told her that he didn't want to hear any information second hand.

The visit at the health department was not long. They were in and out. The physician let them know that no news is good news. It simply meant that if they were not contacted, there was no need to worry. They only needed to worry if any form of contact was made, be it in a form of letter or phone call. They immediately left the health department and headed for the court building. Finding a parking space was no problem. Andre was able to park in the front of the courthouse. After going through the metal detectors, they reached the elevator of the Federal Court building. Andre looked around to see if he saw any of his fellow officers.

The bell rang and they boarded the elevator. The doors opened right to the courtroom in which they were going. Andre held the door open as Asia entered the room; she looked for a place to sit, a voice caught her attention as he said, "I do."

Asia noticed her Uncle Rob as he let his right hand down to take a seat. She wanted to know what her uncle had to do with this situation that had Andre so paranoid about. Andre had noticed Robert way before Asia. As she looked for a seat, he had his eyes on Robert, while he tried to keep up with Asia's movements.

Asia had her eyes directly on Robert. He was smiling at someone. When he winked his eye, Asia followed his eyes. He was staring at a familiar face. Her uncle was admiring a face that Asia hadn't seen since she was five years old. Janice simply smiled back at her brother. At that moment, he found some peace. He had a clean feeling as his chest began to tighten. His adrenaline began to race. He was trying to grasp for the small amount of oxygen that was feeling his lungs. Right when he felt the flow of air, it was as though his oxygen supply was being shut off. Robert's attorney turned to ask him a question and notice the bit of excitement coming from his client's eyes. It appeared that he had seen something disturbing. "Someone call the paramedics!" he quickly screamed as he ran to his aid.

Robert dropped his balled fist from his chest and let out a sigh. He had a massive heart attack before he even had a chance to speak his peace. Asia got up and walked toward her mother. Asia looked her in her eyes and began to cry. She never imagined that her wish would come true. Asia tried to gather the right words that she wanted to say. Nothing could come out. She couldn't even speak.

Everything in the courtroom became frantic. The spectators were moving about. Their whispers were filling the room. The judge began to bang his gravel and yell, "Order in this court! Order I say!" The whole scene was chaotic. There was a lot of commotion taking place and a lot of movement going on. The judge was being ignored. The one thing that mattered to Janice would never be answered. This was her only reason for showing up. She thought she was about to find out what truly happened, despite the lies and the rumors she once heard. She gathered herself and began to walk out the courtroom.

Andre looked over to Asia. Her face was filled with disappointment. From the look in her eyes, he knew something wasn't right. Asia was fixated on something. He followed to where her eyes were directed. For a minute, he felt Asia was walking out of the courtroom. There was a slight resemblance to the figure about to exit the courtroom doors. He watched as the woman that Asia resembled, was now strolling out of the courtroom. Asia was lost for words as she stood there in disbelief. She placed her head in her hands and closed her eyes. Opening her eyes, she noticed the room full of armed officers.

She let out a deep sigh. Closing her eyes, she could feel her body standing up. As she exited the courtroom, she looked at an officer standing close to the exit door. She walked passed him and brushed up against him. He was so focused on all the commotion taking place he didn't realize that Asia had lifted his piece.

Right outside the courthouse, she saw her mother standing on the steps near the sidewalk of the court building. She was standing with her back to the doors. Asia couldn't tell what her mother was doing. She observed her as she wondered just what she was going to say to her. Once she got all the way outside, she saw that her mother taking a puff from her cigarette.

Asia walked up to her with her hands behind her back. She stood their staring very hard at her mother. She didn't realize how much she resembled her mother. She thought she was looking at herself in the mirror. She knew exactly how she would look once she aged. She was trying to think of the words she wanted to say but she couldn't come up with anything. She didn't know what to address her as. For years, she dreamed up having the opportunity to get some things off her chest that involved her mother.

Asia began to cry, "You know I have seen a lot of stars. Each time I was waiting on a star to fill the void that I had. It never happened. Then today I lose the one person that I know as family, and I don't think you even deserve to be here." Asia moved her hands from behind her back. She realized the reason that she tried so hard to delete the memories of her mother. To her, Janice died a long time ago. She didn't understand how she stood before her and not even acknowledge she was there. Her mother had a cold look in her eyes. She looked every bit of a scorned woman. Asia was trying to figure out; was it something she had done?

"Do you love me? Have you ever loved me? Did you wonder about what I was going through without you in my life? Did you even think about who was going to tell me about my menstruation, boys, sex, and life? Did you even care about how I was going to determine myself worth?" Asia eyes were filled with a watery liquid. She became so angry that her mother didn't respond.

Janice stood as if she was a deaf mute. She was making love to the cigarette. She was so into her cancer stick that she didn't realize that she was at the butt of it and it had been all smoked up. The flames sizzled as it reached its end. She must have noticed that the cigarette was at its near end. She slowed down her puffs trying to make the little that was left last. There was no more; she had to throw it down. Before she released it, she was trying to find something else to focus on as she looked out in the action that was taking place. News reporters were flooding the area. Traffic remained at a steady place. Pedestrians were crossing at the intersection without a care in the world. A couple sat under the tree. Individuals were freely coming and going in the court building.

Asia could remember the green Nova as it pulled up in front of her uncle's home. When she knocked on that door to go in, she didn't realized that she was going to grow up in that very house without the mother who had given birth to her. She never had the chance to ask about her father. She wanted to know his likes and his dislikes. In the back her mind, she realized that she now had the opportunity to ask her mother all the unanswered questions she had. That's when she came to her conclusion. She hadn't learned all that she wanted about her parents, so there was no need now. She pointed the officer's revolver at her mother, "Tell me one thing you have worth living for!"

Janice stood there puffing away at her next cigarette. She glanced at Asia for a silent moment. She turned her lips and flickered her eyes. Once the movements of her body parts ceased, she continued, to make love to her cigarette. She had no reason to live. Asia would be doing her a favor.

Bang! Bang! Bang! Bang! Bang! Bang! Bang! Bang! Bang! The bullets rippled through Janice's body. Asia looked around in amazement. She had not pulled the trigger but someone else had. She scanned the area and noticed another face that she hadn't seen in years. Asia turned back to look at her mother. She looked down at her mother as she lie in a puddle of blood.

Asia fell to her knees and profusely began to shake nervously. She didn't think she had the gained the courage to take her mother's life. She wanted her mother to become frantic, apologetic, and then beg for her life. When she grabbed the gun from the officer, her plan was to use it to make her mother stick around and discuss why she left her in the first place. Now that she lie drenched in blood, she didn't know what or how she was feeling. At that moment, she felt as though she had just observed a stranger that had been harmed.

She had managed to make it this far without her. All she ever wanted was an understanding. She wanted to know who Janice really was and why she wasn't there to show her any love and affection. In the back of her mind, she felt that she was some sort of bad curse. She didn't have time to complain because Shante filled that void. Shante not only understood her but she enjoyed her as they enjoyed each other's company. Asia was able to swallow the fact that she had been abandoned and she missed out on that mother daughter relationship; the type of relationship that grows into a friendship; a type of friendship that is developed due to having a loving parent.

The dispatcher was coming across the police scanners. The officers listened to a disturbance-taking place right outside the court building. Extra officers had already come to see what disturbance occurred in the courtroom. Several officers began to disperse from the courtroom and make their way to the crime scene. Andre looked around and noticed that Asia was nowhere in sight. He rushed outside and saw Asia kneeling down by woman who Asia resembled.

Andre went to her side and wrapped his arms around her. He watched as her Aunt Wanda was being handcuffed and escorted away. When Wanda was being placed in the back of the police car, she looked over at Asia. Wanda gave Asia a little wink and smiled. She laid her back as though she could finally relax because she had finally had the opportunity to tie up some loose ends.

Asia and Andre watched as the police car drove off into the distance. She didn't know that Wanda had that in her. She wanted to be mad at Wanda for taking the opportunity from her. That was not what Wanda had planned. When she saw Asia with the weapon behind her back, she didn't want her to through her life away on someone that didn't deserve it. She was coming for the man who robbed her of her life, but that had been taking care of.

The paramedics rushed to the scene. Blood was lunging from her body. Her blouse was drenched. It didn't even look as though the paramedics had stabilized her. An oxygen mask was placed on her face. Janice was quickly placed on the stretcher. Asia laid her head on Andre's chest. He stood with a look of bewilderment. As Asia was crying a river, the tears drenched his shirt.

"Come on and pull yourself together so that we can go to the station and see about your Aunt Wanda." Andre kissed Asia on her forehead and she began walking beside him. By the time she reached the car, she had calmed down. Andre opened her car door. She entered the car and he shut the door once she was situated, he ran around to the driver's side and got in.

They made it to the police station. Asia trailed behind Andre as he entered the doors. He instructed Asia to go sit in the waiting area. Asia walked over to the cushioned seats that were in the waiting area. The local news was covering the high profile case in which the chief of police was involved. Asia was on her way over to the vending machine when she was interrupted with the breaking news from the newscaster.

"Find out why an unidentified woman was slain right outside the court building where the chief of police was having his preliminary hearing. Tune in, this is some news you don't want to miss." The newscaster stated immediately followed by a commercial.

Andre walked into the waiting area. He looked into Asia's weeping eyes. She was sitting looking off as if she were in a trans. Andre walked over and knelt down in front of her, "I made arrangements for you to go back and talk to your aunt." He grabbed a hold of both of her hands, "It's really up to you. If you don't want to go back no one will make you."

Tilting her head to the side, all she could do was smile, as she looked upon her longtime friend's face. It's was this very moment that she realized why she cared so much for him. He showed a lot of passion when he spoke and looked into her eyes. Asia stood up and took a very deep breath, "Andre, I haven't seen or heard from her in a very long time. We didn't have a close nit bond at all. I really need to know why she would do that to my mother. Besides you and Shante, Wanda is the only family member that I have left. She has to have a reason for what she has done."

Asia followed Andre to where Wanda was being held. She was in a small room with a very large steal table. She was sitting were a prisoner would be handcuffed to the floor and table but she was not in any handcuffs or leg irons. Asia walked over to her and gave her a hug. She was not the oversized woman she once was. She wasn't very small or very big. She was in between and on the borderline of thick.

Asia stood back, "You looking good these days. Too bad Uncle Rob didn't have the opportunity to see you."

Wanda searched to see the hidden emotions of Asia. She grinned and let out a small chuckle.

One tear began to roll down Asia's face, "Wanda can you tell me why you just shot my mother?"

Wanda knew that was the reason for Asia coming to see her. She stood and grabbed of hold of Asia's hand, "Asia I had no intentions of bringing harm to your mother today. I was coming to see how this trial would end up and what would happen to your uncle. Then I bumped into you and your mother. I overheard you asking her, "Why." When she didn't answer, I just felt as though she didn't need to be around to bring anyone anymore sorrow. You and I both buried her a long time ago and I didn't want you to have to hurt anymore.

You needed to be set free."

Asia studied her as she spoke. She tried to understand everything she was saying. Andre moved in to hold Asia. Asia's body flinched very quickly. Andre could tell that she was becoming very weak in the knees. Asia closed her eyes and bowed her head. The room was very quiet. There was no sound that could be heard throughout the police department. It was as though someone had picked up a remote control and pressed mute.

Asia looked at Wanda, "I pray she lives because I wasn't done talking to her. You are not the higher power that can make that type of decision. Do know that I am not angry with you at all. You abandoned me too. To make matters worse you even stole from me. Then you come here and try to steal the one chance I get to know why my mother did what she did to me. She might not have answered then, but eventually she might have answered had you allowed her that opportunity. Yes, I do forgive you."

Asia turned to Andre so that they could leave the room. Andre embraced her. He looked into her eyes, "Asia, I am going to love you for the rest of my days. I am going to love you and treat you the way someone should have treated my daughter." He placed a kiss on her forehead.

Asia tightly squinted her eyes. She was overwhelmed from confusion. She must have heard him wrong and he must have meant something else. They exited the police station and, "My Daughter", repeatedly played over in over in Asia's mind as if it were a scratch on a CD that made the statement keep repeating. She was fighting with her thoughts and what Andre had just said to her.

"He had to be thinking of the future in hopes that he will have a daughter and he wants her to be treated with the up most respect." Asia glanced at him as he drove, "He must have meant that he is going to treat me the way he would want someone to treat his daughter because after all, I am not Washed Up I am some man's daughter."

Andre approached the intersection. He could feel Asia's eye's piercing through to his soul. He was not trying to say what had so naturally rolled off his tongue. He wanted to look at Asia to see if anything was biting away at her, but he was fighting with his own lies. This was the time to move forward and there was no reason to look back. All that she did in her past would remain there. He was not about to let a piece of paper change his views. If he didn't know anything else, he knew that no one would love him the way Asia did. He knew that she had come to the point in her life where she was ready to have him change her last name.

Asia leaned her head back on the headrest. She decided against asking him anything. There was nothing she was going to worry about. As long as he kept it real and knew that there was, going to be no more secrets everything would be cool. From this day forward, she was going to remain true to him. She knew exactly what she was going to do. The past was going to be just that, The Past. She was trying to spend the rest of her life with him. It was just two little words that mattered. I DO!

Chapter 27

IT WAS ALL A DREAM

"You missed a beautiful sermon today." Shante told Asia when she called to make sure that she would be at the airport to pick her and Andre up.

"I know girl, but this was worth the trip. I got the chance to network with so many fashion designers. Even Kimora was in the place, but I didn't have the chance to converse with her, but maybe next time." Asia filled her in on the rest of her trip as Andre gathered their items so they could catch their taxi.

When Asia finally got the call and the invitation to show off her exclusive bleached and lightly faded denim jeans at the Waldorf-Astoria, Shante wanted to be there for her like her left hand. Shante hated that Aaron was having his custody hearing when her friend was ripping the runway in New York.

The taxi took the scenic route getting them to LaGuardia Airport. Asia couldn't miss another flight because the show for her débuting her new jean line was the next day. She and Andre raced through the central terminal once they were passed all the security checkpoints. Asia sat on the plane thinking about how she had spoke with the owner of the Loft Nightclub. She had convinced him to let her do a fashion show as the opening to the mini-concert he was having for the local rapper back-to-school charity event. The first thing on her list was to call up the twelve models that would be modeling her line. Then she was going to call Paul and thank him for always encouraging her.

When he invited her to his church, his Bishop had preached a sermon that had a heavy message based on one having hope, courage and faith. With all that it lead to her pursing that dream and in a few hours she would be living out her dream as part owner of a new jean line *Washed Up* would be hitting the runway in her hometown.

The event put Asia over the top. She and Shante took pictures with all the locals. Andre and Aaron just played the background. The models even got in a few pictures displaying their lightly low rise faded denim jeans with *Washed UP* stamped on the back right side at the top of the jean.

Aaron and Shante prepared to leave. They said their goodbyes and catch up with you laters as they embraced one another with love. Asia couldn't stop smiling she waved as the two exited the building. Andre let her know he had to drain the weasel. Asia sat at the bar gazing at her wedding ring while Andre made a pit stop at the restroom.

Asia sat their patiently thinking about all that came out to support her. She tickled herself thinking about Shante insisting on wearing her new jeans and being whole lot different from everyone else's, but Asia couldn't resist putting the hand prints on the derriere. She lost her thoughts as she heard conversation approaching her. The lights were bright because the workers were now cleaning up the establishment. She could smell the money as two people approached her. She looked up and seen the delicate eyes, nicely trimmed goatee, and the dreads that were freshly pulled back. Asia thought to herself, *"Mr. Gwop getta in the flesh!"* She didn't even notice the other person and he was sporting some bright lime green from head to toe.

"Where can I pick up a pair of those jeans?" the person wearing a diamond bezzled platinum chain with Derrty hanging from it asked.

Asia smiled and batted her eyes. She could hear Shante saying, "Asia, don't hurt'em, girl!" She couldn't believe that this *lunatic* was asking her about her clothing line.

"Gone put this number in yo phone, then you can call me and I can come pick me some up."

Asia didn't know why he even wanted some denim jeans designed only for females, but she didn't hesitate putting his number in her phone. She didn't even take a minute to look around to see if her husband was in the vicinity. When she finished he and the fellow wearing lime green walked away. She was watching his every move. Before he reached the door, he turned to say, "I didn't even tell you my name!"

He smiled as he yelled from the door, "It's Murph!"

ORDER FORM

Red Bud Ave Publications
P. O. BOX 6227
St. Louis, MO 63106

Name: _______________________________________

Address: _____________________________________

City/State: ___________________________________

Zip: ____

QUANTITY	TITLES	PRICES
	Washed UP	$15.00
	Taylor Made	$15.00
	Simply Taylor Made	$15.00
	Tales From the Lou	$15.00
	Total	$____________